A Boy and His Bear

"I'd not have believed it unless I'd seen it with my own eyes," he continued.

"Before I could get to the lad, the she-bear went up on her hind legs. I thought he was done for then, I can tell you, lying like a stone on the ground. But the cub was having none of it. It gave a growl, and –"

"Aye?"

"And jumped between her and the lad. Stopped her…" He paused, looking down at Dickon, his craggy face puzzled. The he shook his head. "I tell you, Master, 'twas the strangest thing I ever did see."

D0543215

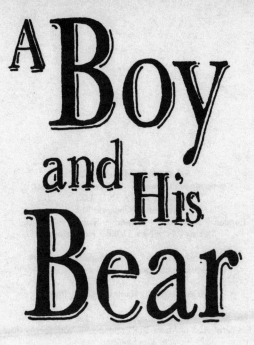

A Boy and His Bear

Harriet Graham

Scholastic Children's Books,
Commonwealth House, 1–19 New Oxford Street,
London WC1A 1NU, UK
a division of Scholastic Ltd
London ~ New York ~ Toronto ~ Sydney ~ Auckland
Mexico City ~ New Delhi ~ Hong Kong

First published in the UK by Scholastic Ltd, 1994
This edition published by Scholastic Ltd, 1996

Text copyright © Harriet Graham, 1994

The Bells of Heaven by Ralph Hodgson has been included
by kind permission of Macmillan London Ltd., with special thanks
to Mrs Hodgson.

ISBN 0 590 13365 9

Typeset by DP Photosetting, Aylesbury, Bucks.
Printed by Cox & Wyman Ltd, Reading, Berks.

10 9 8 7 6 5 4

The right of Harriet Graham to be identified as the author of this work has been
asserted by her in accordance with the Copyright, Designs and Patents Act,
1988.

The Bells of Heaven

'Twould ring the bells of Heaven
The wildest peal for years,
If Parson lost his senses
And people came to theirs,
And he and they together
Knelt down with angry prayers
For tamed and shabby tigers
And dancing dogs and bears,
And wretched, blind pit ponies,
And little hunted hares.

Ralph Hodgson

"This day I saw Harry Hunks, a blind and weeping
bear whipped by six men until the blood ran down his
shoulders."

Visitor to London in the sixteenth century

For Adam, my brother and kindred spirit.

Prologue

IN THE BEGINNING...

At first there is only warmth and the smell of milk; then finding the milk in the warm darkness and drinking, and sleeping again. Next time I wake my mother washes me. I feel her tongue, hear the noise it makes as it moves over my fur. She grunts. Go to sleep again, little bear. I sleep.

Time passes. Time comes when I open my eyes, close them, open them again. Now I can see the cave which is our home; in the shadows the darker shadow of my mother beside me. Light comes from the opening. Beyond the opening there is a new sound. Something is howling. I am afraid. My mother pushes me close to her with her nose ... grunts ... all is well, little bear ... sleep again.

There is the dark time and the light time. In the dark time the birds do not sing. Sitting at the edge of the cave I watch them as they fly from tree to tree. When the dark time is near they fly up to the high branches and stay there until the light time comes back. In the dark time there is the baying of wolves and the screech of the owl as she hunts for food. My mother grunts when she hears the wolves, pushes me close under her with her nose. We are safe in our cave.

I am strong now. I climb on my mother's back and bite her ears. If I bite too hard she cuffs me with her paw. When she goes away from the cave I sit and wait for her. She has gone hunting. Soon I am strong enough to hunt with her. My mother shows me how to move the earth under the trees with my paws, to stand up beside the tree and catch the good things that hide there. I can climb the trees myself now. My claws are strong and dig into the bark as I go up, up. When the dark time comes we go back to the cave. When the wet time comes and the water falls from the sky it is good to go fishing. I learn how to scoop the fish out of the water with my paws. The water does not hurt me because I can swim in it. Then I shake it off, and the bright light in the sky dries me.

Now I am afraid of nothing except the wolves that hunt at night and the snakes that lie asleep in the long grass. I am strong and the forest is mine. None can harm me. None except the beast that walks on two legs. He is more cunning than I am. More cunning even than my mother is.

We are in the cave. The beast with two legs is near us, and I am afraid. But my mother tells me to lie still … then the beast will not find us … do not fear, little bear, see … the beast has gone away…

Now the beast has come back, and this time he has brought fire. Our cave is full of smoke. My mother starts to dig. We dig a hole that will take us out of the cave, out into the clean air. Dig, little bear, dig! We climb up through the hole, out into the forest…

But the beast with two legs is waiting for us. He has a net. My mother fights with him. She snaps and bites and growls, but it is no use. We are trapped.

Then the beast with two legs lifts us up and throws us into a dark place that moves. He is taking us away from the forest, my mother and I.

Chapter One

Somewhere a bell was clanging.
Di-dang, di-dang, di-dang.

It was the start of another day at Master Nashe's tannery in Twill Lane, and Mistress Nashe, heaving on the bellrope with her rolling-pin arms, glanced up at the attic window under the eaves.

"Six of the clock and a fine, bright day," she sang out above the clamour of the bell.

Upstairs in the bed he shared with his fellow apprentice, Dickon, who had nothing to look forward to on that day or any other day, pulled the blanket over his ears to shut out the sound and tried to burrow back inside his dream. A good dream it was, with his father in it, and his father's grey mare, and a line of blue hills that they were setting off to ride to, and beyond the blue hills the promise of something exciting and mysterious.

Then the clanging stopped, and Dickon felt the

creak and sway of the bed and heard the thump of Ned's feet on the attic boards. He screwed his eyes tight shut. But it was no use, the dream had gone.

"You'll be last at the pump again," Ned said, giving him a shake. "And last to table. That'll be the fourth time this week, Dickon."

With a groan Dickon pushed back the blanket and rolled out of bed. Ned had his tunic on already and was pulling at his stockings and Peter and Gilbert, the two older apprentices, were fully dressed. Dickon grabbed at his tunic.

"Wait for me," he said. "Just this once, Ned … please."

"Then I'll be last," Ned grinned.

"We could go together," Dickon said, pulling on his stockings. "Look, I'm almost ready."

But Ned had pushed on his shoes and was following the two older boys towards the door.

"I woke you up, didn't I?" he said over his shoulder.

It was true, Dickon thought. Ned had to wake him most mornings. Sometimes he didn't even hear the bell. It was no wonder he was always last at the pump. Reaching for his shoes, Dickon shivered, thinking of the day that stretched ahead, and of Mistress Nashe's shrill, scolding voice. He wished he could climb back into bed, pull the blanket over his head and wake up somewhere amongst the blue hills of his dream.

It wasn't that he was lazy, although Mistress Nashe told him often enough that he was. At school he had worked hard at his books, and had done well. But those had been good days, before he was apprenticed to Master Nashe. So good that Dickon tried not to think too much of them now, for this was a different time, and he was a different person, or so it seemed to him.

Then he had lived with his mother and father and his sister, Ann, in the tall, gabled house by the river. Dickon's father was a merchant, trading in furs and fine cloth and gem stones, and from the Pool of London his travels took him across to France, to Flanders and Italy; once as far as Russia. When he returned from one of his journeys he would come striding up the street with his servant Jacob struggling along behind him, quite loaded down with all the luggage. Never a journey but he brought back presents for them all . . . fine cloth and jewelled capes for Dickon's mother and Ann, and for Dickon all manner of wonderful things. Once it was a little sledge from Flanders, painted in scarlet and green; another time a hoop that he could bowl along. But best of all was the carved wooden flute that his father had brought him from Germany. Dickon had taught himself to play it, and before long he could pick out the songs he heard in the streets and the melodies of Wales that his mother sang.

"That's the Welsh blood in you," his mother had told him proudly. "In Wales there is music wherever you go."

"You and your Welsh blood," his father had laughed. "Music is all very well, but Latin and Greek will stand Dickon in better stead."

Dickon's mother wasn't listening, though. She was remembering the green valleys she had left behind when she came to London to marry, and Ann, seeing her look sad, had laid down her sewing and asked her father to go on with the story he was telling them about his latest journey.

And then, one hot summer's day in July everything had changed. On that day, Dickon's father had not come striding up the street as they had seen him do so often, but had walked slowly, like an old man, holding fast to Jacob's arm, his face as grey as ashes. Long before he reached their door Dickon could see that he was shaking with the fever that had taken hold of him. Within three days he was dead. He left debts behind him, too, and no money to pay them with, so the fine gabled house by the river had to be sold, and Dickon and his mother and Ann had moved into lodgings. They were poor then, but at least they had all been together.

Until Master Tyndal the butcher began to call. At first it was once a week, then twice a week, then every day, and within a year Dickon's mother had married again and the family had moved into Master Tyndal's home above the butcher's shop in East-cheap.

The house was a brooding, silent place, and Dickon was glad to leave it each day and go to school. His mother had changed since her marriage to Master Tyndal. She no longer laughed or sang the songs of Wales as she used to, and her red-gold hair which Dickon's father had been so proud of because it was the colour of the great Queen's hair, was becoming streaked with grey. Ann was quieter, too, and spent most of her day embroidering jewelled gloves which she sold to the tailor in Eastcheap. Even Jacob, their father's old servant, had left them, and before long there was a new baby, a whining thing called Luke, that lay in the cradle beside his mother. Dickon felt more lonely than ever.

Master Tyndal was a short, round man with a clean shaven face and large hands forever sawing the air, so that even when he sat at table he still seemed to be cutting up meat in the shop. For Dickon and Ann he had few words, and as the months passed his small watchful black eyes turned more and more often towards Dickon, until one day, coming home from school Dickon overheard him talking to his mother.

"Better the boy is apprenticed and learn an honest trade," he said. "All this book learning will do him little good."

Dickon had stood very still, trying to catch his mother's answer, but the baby started to cry and he could hear no more.

The very next day his stepfather had taken him to meet Master Nashe at the tannery in Southwark.

Dickon knew at once that he didn't want to be apprenticed to Master Nashe. The very sight and smell of the place made him sick.

"You'll grow used to it soon enough, boy," Master Nashe said, seeing the look on Dickon's face as he stared at the line of carcasses which hung head down, on hooks from the beam. "The beasts are dead, after all. They'll not bite."

Dickon watched the blood dripping on to the ground and said nothing.

"I tell you what it is," his stepfather said, his voice

smooth. "All this book learning has turned the boy into a milksop. Hard, honest labour is what he needs."

"He'll get plenty of that in my yard," Master Nashe nodded. "Still ... a milk sop, eh? Is that what you are, lad?"

"Not I," Dickon flashed. "I like animals... I like –"

"You'd best like them since they're to be your livelihood," Master Nashe said, clapping him on the shoulder, and he looked at Master Tyndal and laughed. Dickon had meant that he liked live animals, but it was too late to explain for at that moment Mistress Nashe put her head round the door. "The new apprentice," Master Nashe told her, his hand still on Dickon's shoulder.

Mistress Nashe looked Dickon up and down, wiping her arms on her apron.

"He's very thin," she said. "And his hair, it's very red."

"Book learned, too, I'm told," Master Nashe said.

"Book learned?" Mistress Nashe snorted. "Well, there'll be no time for that here. Hard work is what's wanted."

"And hard work is what he'll get," Master Nashe nodded. "In six years," he went on, turning to

Master Tyndal, "I'll turn this milksop of yours into the finest Master Tanner this side of the Thames."

"Except for yourself, of course," Master Tyndal said drily, and they both laughed.

Six years, Dickon thought, staring at the line of animals, as his stepfather and Master Nashe shook hands on the bargain they had made. Six years... The pigs had their eyes shut, but the sheep stared sadly at the ground as though being dead and hanging there was a great surprise to them. Six years ... it might as well have been sixty.

Master Tyndal hummed a little tune to himself as they walked back across London Bridge. It was the only time Dickon ever heard him sing.

It was past noon when they arrived back at the house in Eastcheap, and Ann and his mother were sitting in the upper room.

"Well, that's settled," Master Tyndal said. "The lad starts at the tannery the day following May Day."

Dickon saw the troubled, questioning look that Ann gave his mother and knew that at least she would be on his side.

"I'm sure Dickon is very grateful," his mother said timidly. "Aren't you, Dickon?"

"Grateful or not I warrant you it will do him more

good than squinting over those books," Master Tyndal said, not waiting for Dickon's answer.

When he had gone Dickon's mother held out her hand to him.

"'Tis a great chance for you, Dickon," she said.

"'Tis no chance at all," Dickon blurted out in sudden rage. "To be a tanner, to work all day with dead animals . . . for SIX YEARS . . . I would sooner be dead myself."

"Don't speak so," his mother cried. "You must see that your stepfather thinks only of what is best for you. He is a good man, Dickon. He is paying out of his own pocket for you to learn an honest trade."

Dickon said nothing to that. He remembered how Master Tyndal had sung as they crossed London Bridge, and he thought his stepfather was glad to pay the money so that he would not have to see him every day.

Ann shook her head.

"Dickon is right," she said, putting down the glove she was embroidering and giving her mother an earnest look. "The tannery is no life for him. To leave his books when he is doing so well. . ." She frowned. "It is not what father would have wanted. You know it isn't."

For a moment a look of doubt crossed his mother's face. Then she tightened her lips.

"Things are different now," she said, her voice growing suddenly harder. "Dickon has a new father and must do as he directs. As we all must." And bending over the cradle she picked up the whining Luke and rocked him in her arms.

Dickon saw then how it was. His father's hopes and dreams for him were quite finished. His step-father had seen to that. His mother would not take his side, and Ann, who understood well enough how he felt, could do nothing.

Four months had gone by since then, and as each unending day went drearily past Dickon grew to hate his life at the tannery more and more. Only on Sunday afternoons could he escape. Then, with the other apprentices, he had leave to go out after the midday dinner until curfew sounded. The few, precious hours sped past all too swiftly, and then another week lay ahead, another week of drudgery and ugliness and stink, and Mistress Nashe never far off with her bullying and scolding. Things wouldn't be so bad if it weren't for Mistress Nashe, Dickon thought. But she seemed to have taken a dislike to him the very first time she set eyes on him, and gave him no peace.

She was waiting for him that morning when he reached the yard.

"Here comes our snail, our little slug-a-bed," she bellowed, grabbing Dickon and pushing him roughly under the pump.

Dickon winced and gritted his teeth as the freezing water gushed over his head. He had learnt that there was no point in wriggling or protesting. The trick was to stay still and try to get his head as far under the spout of water as possible; that way it didn't run down inside his collar. The dousing seemed to last longer than ever that day, though, and between the clank of the pump and the rush of the water Dickon could hear Mistress Nashe's litany "...snail, slug-a-bed, lazy, good for nothing wastrel..." until at last, worn out with the effort, she let go of him.

"There. Now get inside to the table," she panted.

Shaking the water from his hair and ears, Dickon shot away from her. Mistress Nashe followed him into the kitchen, still wiping her arms on her apron, and began to cut hunks of barley bread from the loaf. The others were already at the table and Dickon wished that he could slide on to the bench beside Ned, as far away from Mistress Nashe as possible. But as the youngest apprentice it was his place to hand round the food, so he must needs stand and wait while she piled the slices of bread into the trencher and poured out the beer. The exercise at the pump had brought a brick red flush to her face, and beads of perspiration stood out on her nose and upper lip as she hacked at the loaf. Dickon stood very still, watching the kitchen cat twine itself around her skirts. He was fond of the cat, and sometimes fed it with titbits from the table when no one was watching. Once it had made its way up to the attic and slept all night curled in the crook of his arm.

Mistress Nashe kicked the cat out of the way and shoved the trencher of bread towards Dickon.

"Don't stand there day dreaming, Carrot Head," she said. "Hand that round."

Dickon felt his stomach tighten into an angry knot. More than anything he hated it when she called him Carrot Head. If only she would leave him alone. But Mistress Nashe hadn't finished with him yet.

"Don't think you're going to get away with it," she went on, her voice rising again. "Last on Monday, last on Tuesday, last on Wednesday ... and now, last on Thursday. You've been nothing but trouble ever since you came here, and this time," she said, banging the beer pitcher down so hard on the table that even Peter and Gilbert stopped talking and looked up, "this time Master Nashe will hear of it. A good beating is what you need, Carrot Head, and I'm going to see that you get it."

Dickon slid on to the bench beside Ned, and sat, staring at the ridges on the scrubbed wooden table. So far he had escaped being beaten, but he had seen the evil looking cane that Master Nashe kept in the corner of the workshop and the thought of it filled him with dread. Opposite him, Peter and Gilbert tore at their bread, stuffing handfuls into their mouths, and swilling it down noisily with their beer. But Dickon could eat nothing that morning, knowing what lay in store for him.

After a while Mistress Nashe went over to the fire and began rattling with the pots and pans.

"Don't worry," Ned whispered, nudging him in the ribs. "You'll see, she'll forget once her anger's cooled."

Ned had been the youngest apprentice until Dickon arrived, and had had his share of kicks and cuffs from Mistress Nashe. But Dickon shook his head.

"She'll not forget," he muttered. "She hates me."

"I wager she will," Ned whispered, wiping his sleeve across his mouth. After a moment he nudged

Dickon again. "You going to eat that?" he asked, jerking his thumb towards the two pieces of bread. "Because if you don't want it. . ."

But at that moment Master Nashe appeared in the doorway. It was the signal to start work, and for the moment at least luck was on Dickon's side, for Mistress Nashe was still clattering with the fire and didn't see him. Pushing half his bread towards Ned and stuffing the other piece into the pocket of his tunic, Dickon slid quickly off the bench.

In the workshop, Peter and Gilbert pulled back the bolts on the great double doors and swung them open, letting in the early September sunshine. Dickon fetched the broom and began to sweep up the soiled straw from the floor. This was his first task each day. Next he must fetch clean straw from the hay loft and scatter it thickly so that it covered the beaten earth. Usually this was the part of the morning he liked best, for the smell of the straw reminded him of the stable at home, where his father's mare had stamped and whinnied in its box while Jacob, whistling softly as he worked, groomed the grey, dappled coat to a rich shine. But that morning Dickon thought only of the beating to come, and whichever way his eyes turned the cane seemed to be always in view.

When he had swept the straw into a heap he straightened up. Through the open door he could see Master Nashe out in the yard, talking to the carter who had brought a fresh load of carcasses. Mistress Nashe was with him. Dickon propped the broom up against the wall, his heart beating fast. For the moment they had their backs to him. If he could just reach the hay loft without being seen, he thought, he could slip inside and stay out of sight for a while.

Cautiously he edged round the doorway and set off.

He had nearly reached the hay loft when he tripped over a bucket, and fell, sprawling full length on the ground. Master Nashe was beside him in an instant, and Dickon felt himself being hauled to his feet.

"You, boy," Master Nashe boomed. "I want you. You're to come with me."

Chapter Two

Dickon's head was still singing from the fall he had taken as Master Nashe marched him back through the double doors into the workshop, and he stared straight ahead, his heart pounding at the thought of the beating that would shortly come. There was no escape from it now. He knew that.

But Master Nashe didn't stop to pick up the cane. Instead, his hand still firmly grasping Dickon's collar, he strode without a word towards the counting house at the back of the workshop and, opening the door, pushed Dickon inside.

"Stay there until I come back, and don't stir," he growled.

Left to himself, Dickon took a deep breath, rubbed the bruise on his elbow and looked about him.

He had never been in the counting house before, though he had seen Master Nashe's clerk who worked there, a thin old man with wisps of white hair straggling out from under his shiny skull cap, who sometimes pattered noiselessly through the work-shop, returning a few moments later with a mug of ale and a piece of bread and cheese, and closing the door behind him again. But the clerk was not there that morning, and Dickon was alone in the long, low-ceilinged room. In the centre stood a table piled high with papers, and at the far end was a stool, with quill pens and ink and a candle set down before it. The only light came from a small window, criss-crossed with cobwebs through which Dickon could make out the back of the woodshed. Better to be beaten in here than outside in the workshop, in front of the others, he thought, still rubbing his elbow, for the shame of that would be worse than the beating itself. Faintly from the yard he heard the rumble of wheels as the carter left, and then Master Nashe's voice giving some order to Ned.

I would have this over and done with, he thought. The waiting is the worst of all.

But when Master Nashe came back a moment or so later Dickon saw to his astonishment that he had still not brought the cane with him, and instead of the threatening frown that Dickon had expected, Master Nashe gave him a nod.

"Still here, I see," he said.

"Yes, Master," Dickon said. "I'm waiting, as you told me."

"Aye...aye..." Master Nashe nodded, biting at the ends of his moustache. He began to walk up and down, casting sidelong glances at Dickon as he did so and for a while there was silence. "Clerk's at home abed with a fever," he said at last, and waved his hand towards the bench. Dickon frowned. "Well, go on then," Master Nashe said. "Sit down. Take pen and paper. You write a fair hand, don't you, boy? Book learned, so Master Tyndal told me."

Relief flooded over Dickon. There was to be no beating after all.

"Aye, Master, I can write," he said eagerly.

"Well, sit then. And write what I tell you."

Dickon needed no second bidding. This was better than sweeping out the workshop, or spreading down fresh straw, better too than clambering up to the beams to carry down the hides, and better by far than being beaten. This was something that he could do, and do well, and for the first time since he came to the tannery he felt a kind of pleasure in obeying Master Nashe and, smoothing the paper out in front of him, he chose a quill and dipped it in the ink.

"I'd write it myself, only I warrant you'll be faster than me, and I want this delivered before noon,"

Master Nashe said, drumming his fingers on the table. "Are you ready, boy?"

"Yes, Master," Dickon nodded, and bent over the quill to hide his expression, for he had guessed by then that Master Nashe could neither read nor write, and that was why he looked so uncomfortable as he paced up and down the room gnawing at the ends of his moustache.

When the letter was finished Master Nashe came and stood beside the stool, peering over Dickon's shoulder.

"Have you written down everything, boy? Everything that I said?"

"It's all here, Master," Dickon said.

"Well, read it to me then," he commanded. "All of it now. Leave nothing out."

The letter was about some fresh animal hides, how much they would cost and when they could be delivered. When Dickon had finished reading, Master Nashe frowned, biting more savagely than ever at the ends of his moustache.

"Again," he said. "Read it again."

Only after Dickon had read the letter out loud a second time did Master Nashe stop his pacing, and with a satisfied nod walked swiftly to the door. But once there he seemed to change his mind, and turning round he gave Dickon a thoughtful stare and then came back to the table.

"I daresay I can spare you as easily as any of the others," he muttered after a moment's thought. "More easily, maybe."

Dickon's heart beat faster. The day, which had begun so badly, was turning to gold. To be sent out on an errand, away from the tannery, to be free for one precious hour, maybe longer...

"I'll go and willingly, Master," he said quickly, pushing back the stool. "Just tell me where..."

"Not so fast now," Master Nashe growled, watching Dickon roll the letter and tie it with tape. "I've not made up my mind yet. That letter is important. I told you I want it delivered as soon as possible ... no loitering nor stopping at pie shops. Do you hear me, boy?"

"I'll run all the way," Dickon said. "I can run faster than Ned."

"Hmm," said Master Nashe. "Maybe."

"And I'll run all the way back," Dickon added.

"Hmm. Well, see you do. If you're late for midday dinner you'll go hungry till supper time."

"Yes, Master."

"And see here," he went on, catching Dickon by the collar and starting to walk him towards the door, "you're to give the letter to the Master himself. Do you hear me? The Master ... no one else."

"I will," Dickon gasped, "I will ... but –"

"Well?" Master Nashe asked impatiently. "What now?"

"Your pardon, but you haven't told me who the letter is for," Dickon said.

"Why, to the Master of the Bear Pit," Master Nashe roared. "Who else would it be for?" And he shook Dickon once or twice for good measure, and then looked closely at him. "You know where the Bear Garden is, I suppose?"

"On Bankside," Dickon nodded, a little breathlessly. "Hard by the new Globe Theatre."

"Aye, the Globe," Master Nashe growled. "Mark me, now, straight there, and straight back."

They were through the workshop and out in the yard by then. Seeing Dickon with the letter in his hand, Ned's mouth had dropped open, but Dickon paid him no heed. His heart was high at the thought of being beyond the walls of the tannery, and in his mind's eye he was already running towards the river with the wind in his hair. But still Master Nashe held fast to his collar, looking doubtfully at him as though in two minds even now whether to let him go.

"Mark well what I've told you, boy," he said

again, and again Dickon nodded.

"I'm to go as fast as I can to the Bear Garden on Bankside and give this letter to the master ... to no one else."

"Aye, to no one else."

"Then I'm to wait for the answer and bring it back here to you by midday dinner."

"Aye, by midday dinner or earlier," Master Nashe said, still not slackening his grip on Dickon's collar.

"Or earlier," Dickon nodded.

"Hmm," said Master Nashe, and bit the ends of his moustache again. Dickon gave a wriggle.

"The sooner I am gone, Master, the sooner I shall be back," he said.

"Be off with you then," the tanner growled at last, and the next instant Dickon was through the gate and running like the wind.

The morning was bright with warm September sunshine as he sped towards London Bridge, and above the shouts of the merchants calling their wares he could hear the great bell of St Paul's tolling nine o'clock on the far side of the river. Here and there, between the buildings he caught a glimpse of the ships newly docked and riding high at anchor on the tide in the Pool of London, but that morning Dickon was so filled with delight at his sudden freedom that for once he did not long to be down there amongst them, making ready to sail the high seas as he had dreamt so often of doing. It was enough for him that instead of the whipping he had expected he was on his way to the Bear Garden with Master Nashe's letter tucked into the front of his tunic.

The crowd was thicker as he came to London Bridge, and sidestepping a herd of sheep that were being driven in to market, Dickon ducked down the steps that led to St Mary's church, away from the press of people. By cutting through the churchyard he would come to Bankside itself.

He knew the churchyard well, for it was here, on Sunday afternoons, that Ann would come and meet him, taking the ferry across the river from East-cheap. Then they would walk together along the river bank, or sit on the grass sharing the little Sunday cakes that she had made, still warm from baking and wrapped in a napkin. Sometimes she brought a bunch of flowers to put on their father's grave, for he had been born in Southwark and it was here that he was buried. The grass had quite grown over the place now, of course, but the lettering on the stone was still newly chiselled and bold. "Richard Stronge. Merchant of London. Died 6th July in the year of Our Lord 1597."

At fifteen Ann was tall and slender with her father's dark hair and eyes. It was Dickon who had inherited his mother's red hair, which curled around his head like flames.

"You'll get yourself a husband soon," he had teased her only last Sunday as two young men turned to stare at her. One of them even swept off his feathered hat and bowed. "Make sure he's a rich one, Ann."

But Ann had shaken her head.

"Not yet awhile," she said. "I'm needed at home. There will be a new baby in the cradle by New Year, and our mother is not as strong as she was." Dickon had frowned, seeing more clearly than ever why his stepfather had wanted him out of the way, and Ann, understanding how he felt, laid a gentle hand on his arm. "I am welcome still because I can be useful," she said quietly. "That is all. And it is well for you, Dickon, that you are making your own way in the world, even though I know it is hard."

Feeling the familiar anger rise up inside him, Dickon dug his fingers into the moss where they sat.

"Why?" he muttered. "Why did he have to die?"

Ann shook her head and was silent for a moment. Then, jumping up and brushing the grass and twigs from her skirt she held out her hand to him.

"I saw Jacob last week," she said. "He has found new work, at the Globe theatre on Bankside."

Taken by surprise, Dickon had stared at her.

"You mean our Jacob? Our Jacob is an actor?"

"Not exactly." Ann smiled. "He helps in the tiring house, where the actors change into their costumes for the play. And he moves the scenery. You know Jacob ... he can turn his hand to many things."

"Oh I should so like to see him," Dickon said.

"He sent you his greetings," Ann said, "and wondered how you did at your studies."

"And when you told him that I am now apprentice to Master Nashe – what did he say?"

"Not much," Ann said. "Just wrinkled up his face like a sour apple and harrumphed." She did an imitation of him and they both laughed.

Jacob had been part of their family, and Dickon had missed him almost as much as he had missed his father. Many a time, when he was younger, Jacob had carried him on his shoulders to see the great ships at anchor in the Pool of London, and when his sledge ran against a stone step and splintered, it had been Jacob who mended it for him. He had taught him how to whistle, to sharpen a knife on a whetstone and to make oaths in Spanish and French, and the happiest hours that Dickon knew were when, perched on the apple barrel in his father's stable, he had watched Jacob grooming the grey mare and cleaning the harness until the brass shone like gold. The mare had been sold, of course, together with most of their possessions from the tall, gabled house beside the river. All that Dickon had left to remind him of those days was the carved wooden flute his father had given him. That he would never part with. He kept it rolled in a cloth at the bottom of the chest that held his spare clothes, but since he had been at the tannery he hadn't had the heart to play it.

Turning out of the churchyard and on to Bankside, with Master Nashe's letter still tucked securely inside his tunic, Dickon suddenly caught sight of the flagstaff on top of one of the theatres, and stopping for a moment to get his breath back, he was just in time to see the flag being run up. Above the roofs of the houses that lined the river Thames it danced a little, and then, taking the breeze, straightened out and fluttered bravely. Dickon had never been to the play, but he knew that when the flag flew it was to tell the people that there would be a performance put on that day, and his heart lightened to think that Jacob was somewhere there, quite close by. Perhaps, by chance, he might even see him.

To Dickon's right now lay the broad stream of the river where the watermen crossed and re-crossed with their passengers, while to his left there stretched a row of houses and taverns, shoulder to shoulder along the banks of the Thames. Suddenly unsure of which direction to take, he stopped and looked about him.

Nearby a woman was sweeping the steps outside one of the taverns, and going over to her, Dickon asked which was the quickest way to the Bear Garden.

"Another one for the Bear Garden," she exclaimed, resting her broom for a moment and looking Dickon up and down. "It seems every passing stranger needs to know the way there today – or are you 'prentice to that other fellow with the cart?"

"Your pardon, but I am apprentice to Master Nashe the Tanner," Dickon said, "and I have a letter from him for the Master of the Bear Garden. Being in haste –"

"Aye, I'm in haste myself," she cut in. "To finish this sweeping. Only as soon as I pick up the broom along comes someone asking questions. 'Tis the Southwark Fair next week causing all this bustle I shouldn't wonder." She sniffed. "Well, you'd best follow the other. First alleyway past the tavern and go on until you reach the fishponds. You'll see the Bear Garden then, and hear the dogs, too."

"Dogs?" Dickon asked.

"Aye, dogs. The ones they use for the bear baiting," she said, knocking the dust from her broom.

Dickon thanked her and went on.

It was dark in the alleyway after the sunlit brightness of the riverside, and the twisting, overhung roofs that arched above his head blocked out the daylight so that the place seemed close and sinister. There was a foul smell in the air, too, and thinking uneasily that it was a perfect hideout for thieves and cutpurses, Dickon started to run.

He had almost reached the end of the alleyway when he heard the sound of whistling and the rumble of wheels, and coming out suddenly into the sunshine again he saw a covered wagon no more than fifty paces ahead of him, bumping slowly along the path, which ran between cabbage fields towards the Bear Garden.

Dickon could see the round, wooden building, taller than a house and set in open ground where the cabbages petered out. He could hear the baying of dogs too, as the woman had told him he would. He quickened his pace again, tucking the letter more firmly inside his tunic, and before long he had closed the gap between himself and the wagon. The strange, doleful whistling was louder now, although the driver and his horse were still hidden from view by the vast, swaying sides of the wagon. Just as Dickon drew close enough to be able to touch the tail board, the path narrowed, and he had to duck into the cabbage field in order to get past.

It was then, as he drew level with the front of the wagon that he saw the driver for the first time. He was a tall man and dressed from head to heel in the furs of animals, all patched and sewn together into a long surcoat, and his legs, which dangled over the muddy boards, were cross-gartered with strips of fur. On his head he wore a cap, made from the grinning mask of some beast, so that for an instant it seemed to Dickon that the man was not a man at all, but a hideous, two headed ogre from one of the old tales.

Seeing Dickon down below amongst the cabbages staring at him, the man stopped his whistling and his mouth twisted itself into a crooked smile. He would have spoken, but just then there came another sound, a sound unlike anything Dickon had ever heard before, a sound that made the horse begin to throw up its head and plunge in fear, and which sent a sudden shiver down Dickon's spine. It was a deep throated, terrible roar. And it came from somewhere inside the wagon.

Chapter Three

Another instant and Dickon might have taken to his heels, but the man, seeing him still there, was too quick for him.

"Lend us a hand here, young sir," he called down, and the next moment he had jumped off the wagon and thrust the reins into Dickon's hands. Then, brandishing his whip he disappeared round the side of the wagon leaving Dickon to hold the horse.

"Whoa there, whoa," Dickon said quietly, laying his hand on the horse's neck as soon as he could get close enough, for the poor beast was ready to bolt and snorted and rolled its eyes in fear. From the back of the wagon came the sound of the man cursing and beating at something with his whip, until the roars turned to growls; more like a dog now, Dickon thought, as he went on stroking the horse's neck and talking gently to it. But it wasn't a dog. And though the roars had sounded like a bull, it wasn't a bull either. It was no beast that he had ever heard before.

The man came back, tucking the whip into his belt and whistling. There were flecks of blood on his hands, and Dickon liked the look of him less than ever.

"Where are you headed?" he asked, taking the reins from Dickon's hands.

"Over there," Dickon said, pointing towards the Bear Garden, and beginning to back away.

"You can ride with me if you like," the man said, climbing back on the wagon. "If you're not afraid, that is."

"I'm not afraid," Dickon frowned.

"No? Well, hop up then." He held out his hand. Dickon shook his head.

"Thank you, but I'd best run on," he said. "I have an urgent letter for the Master."

"As you like," the man said. "There's not many as will ride with me knowing what it is I carry in my wagon, what it is that roars so." He looked down at Dickon and his mouth twisted into a smile. "You know, don't you?"

Just then the bells began to chime the half hour, and without waiting any longer Dickon started to run. Before he had gone many paces the man's voice floated after him.

"Tell them the Bear Catcher is on his way," he called.

So that was it. In truth he had half known it all along, and he understood now what had made the horse so afraid. The man had brought a fresh supply of bears for the Southwark Fair; there would be baiting then, for sure. Dickon had never seen a bear ... or had he? All at once there came into his mind a memory of being lifted up on his father's shoulders amongst a great crowd of people, and of seeing a huge beast with a rough, brown coat and long claws that walked on its hind legs. And as the beast came on the people fell back, and women screamed in fear. Being safe on his father's shoulders he had not been afraid. He had only felt sorry for the beast and asked why the man whipped it so.

Now, reaching the Bear Garden, Dickon stopped for a moment to catch his breath and stared up at the round, wooden building that was taller than a house. He thought of the bears being led inside to be baited by the dogs, and shuddered. Then, glancing over his shoulder at the wagon which still rumbled steadily forward, he went on again.

There was no one to be seen at the main entrance, but the sound of barking was close now, and seemed to come from the back of the building. Tucking the letter more firmly inside his tunic, Dickon followed the sound, and pushing open a wicket gate found himself in a large yard with outhouses at one end.

Nearby, two men were talking beside one of the heavy posts that stood close to the wall of the main building, and going across to them Dickon asked leave to speak with the Master of the Bear Garden.

"The Master is busy this morning," said the thin faced man. "He expects company shortly – special company." And he winked at his friend.

"The Bear Catcher," Dickon nodded. "That's who you mean, isn't it?"

For a moment the man didn't answer, but watched Dickon through narrowed eyes.

"Maybe," he said at last. "And then again, maybe not."

Dickon looked round the yard. There was no one else about and time was slipping past.

"Please..." he began again. "Will you tell me where to find the Master? I have urgent business with him."

"Urgent business, eh?" the man sneered. "And what might that be, I wonder?"

"It's a letter from my Master, the Tanner," Dickon said, giving the man a straight look. "And before the Bear Catcher arrives I must see the

Master of the Bear Garden. Will you tell me where to find him?"

The fair headed man, who had said nothing until then, unhitched himself from the post at that, and took the straw out of his mouth.

"Don't mind Osric," he said. "I'll take you to the Master. But first – what do you know of the Bear Catcher?"

"Only that I was with him just now, and he said to tell you that he's on his way," Dickon said.

"He's close by then?" the fair haired man asked.

"Halfway across the field when I left him," Dickon nodded. "And now, if you please, my letter. . ."

"Master's coming across the yard now," the man said with a jerk of his head, and he picked up his pail and began to look busy. Turning round Dickon saw a portly figure wearing a fur-trimmed surcoat hurrying towards them.

"Not here yet?" he asked, paying no attention to Dickon.

"Any moment now, Master," the fair haired man nodded. "This young fellow has brought word that he's on his way. And he has a letter for you."

"Most important, so he says," drawled Osric.

"Well?" The Master of the Bear Garden said, turning to Dickon.

"It's from my master," Dickon said, a little breathlessly, pulling the letter out from inside his tunic. "Master Nashe, the Tanner, and he told me to put it into your hand and no one else's."

"Well, give it to me, then, lad," the Master said abruptly, and taking the paper from Dickon he gave a nod and turned back to the fair headed man.

"We shall have our work cut out this morning, Slim," Dickon heard him say. "I want everyone on hand to help. Call up the others ... where's Fulke? And you, Osric, clear the yard and fetch the chains."

The two men ran off towards the outbuildings and the Master would have followed them, only Dickon put out a hand and tugged at his sleeve.

"Well, what now?" the Master frowned. "Can't you see I'm busy here?"

"Begging your pardon, but the letter," Dickon stammered. "My master's orders were that I must bring him back an answer."

"Then you'll have to wait," the Master told him. "You come at a bad moment, lad."

Even as he spoke Dickon heard the approaching rumble of wheels.

"Bear Catcher's here," Osric cried, and suddenly the yard was full of men. Someone swung open the gate and, brushing Dickon to one side and tucking the letter into his belt, the Master strode to meet the wagon.

Seeing him standing in the middle of the yard, Slim came over and took his arm.

"You'd best keep out of the way for the time being," he said. "The beasts will be in an ugly mood this morning."

"But my letter. . ." Dickon protested.

"Later, maybe," Slim said and, stowing Dickon at the far end of the yard by the pump, he ran off again to join the others.

There was nothing for it but to wait, and for a while Dickon forgot the letter as he watched the scene before him.

One of the men had unhitched the horse from the wagon and Dickon saw it being led out of the gate to graze, still snorting with fear at the load it had been pulling. By then six or seven men were gathered around the tail of the wagon. The Bear Catcher was amongst them, Dickon could see that much, but amidst all the shouting and the roaring that came from inside the wagon and the barking of the dogs in their kennels, it was hard to make out what was happening, although Dickon felt certain that before long he would see one of the bears. He stood on tiptoe, ducking his head this way and that to catch a first glimpse of the beast, and his heart was pounding with excitement. Then the shouts grew louder and he saw the Bear Catcher whirl and crack his whip, and from inside the wagon came the first of the bears.

At first all Dickon could make out was a long snout and a brownish mass of fur amongst the men's legs and arms. Then the beast reared itself up on its hind legs, flailing about it with huge claws as the whip fell upon it, and Dickon gasped to see how tall it was ... taller than a man. There were leather thongs around its snout so that it could no longer bite, but still it managed a muffled roar of rage, as with many lashes from the men's whips it was dragged slowly towards one of the posts and chained up.

To begin with, the excitement of seeing the great beast, not fifty paces away from him, was the only thing in Dickon's mind, and he stared in wonder at the sight, watching every movement that the bear made. But as another was led out, and then a third, and as he saw how the men whipped them, and how the poor beasts howled when the lash was laid across their defenceless snouts, a kind of sick sadness crept over him. He stared, still, at the line of beasts but now he pitied them, savage as they were, and sitting down on the edge of the well he closed his eyes for a moment to shut out the sight of the great, shaggy brown animals chained to their posts.

The noise seemed worse than ever then. Dickon wished the dogs would stop their ceaseless barking. And surely the shouting had grown louder.

Opening his eyes again with a start, he saw that the men were in a circle now. Dickon frowned and stood up. Something was there amongst them ... something was moving inside the circle.

Then he saw it. It was a bear, but smaller than the others, not even half grown. Being so small it must have managed to squeeze through the struts of the wagon and run away. Now it pelted round the circle of men, ducking and doubling, until, finding a gap between the legs and whips, it darted through and headed across the yard, straight towards Dickon.

"Watch out there, lad," Slim shouted, as the circle of men wheeled and turned in his direction. "Get back behind the well!"

But Dickon was not afraid. He stood, watching as the cub came on with the men close behind. It was barely ten paces from him when the end of the Bear Catcher's whip caught it as it ran, and with a squeal of pain it fell, rolled over and then sat up at Dickon's feet, panting with terror.

Something of what Jacob had taught him about horses must have come to him at that moment, and feeling nothing but pity for the poor young creature that had run straight to him, he stretched out his hand and laid it gently on the cub's head.

"Poor beast," he murmured.

The cub didn't bite or snap. Instead it stared up at him and gave a kind of shuddering sigh, and Dickon, seeing that it was at the end of its tether with fear and exhaustion, went on standing there, stroking its head.

For a moment they were in a pool of stillness, just him and the bear cub. Then there came the shuffling of feet, and looking up he saw the semicircle of men watching from a little distance, silent and suspicious, as though he had just performed some kind of magic. Only the Bear Catcher smiled his cruel, twisted smile as he shouldered his way through them.

"My thanks again, young sir," he said bending down to fix the rope around the cub's neck. "That's the second time today you've done me a good turn. I'm beginning to think you and I must have been born under the selfsame star," he added softly. Then he straightened up and signalled to the men to drag the bear cub away.

Left alone by the well, Dickon watched them

chain the cub to the wheel of the wagon, away from the other bears. A wave of helpless anger swept over him as he thought of it spending the rest of its life in such a place as this, until at last it ended up in Master Nashe's tannery, hanging upside down from the rafters. He pushed the thought away. There was nothing he could do about it ... nothing. And as though wakening from a dream, he remembered the letter. An hour must have passed since he arrived at the Bear Garden.

"I shall be late for the noonday dinner," he thought, and taking a deep breath he walked quickly across the yard towards the Master, who stood near the wagon, talking to the Bear Catcher. The men turned to stare at him as he passed, but none of them barred his way. When he reached the wagon Dickon stood a little way off, waiting his chance. The two men had their backs to him, studying the row of beasts, but Dickon was close enough now to catch their words.

"No, I tell you, no," the Master said. "What sport is there in a cubling like that? The people will not be pleased. They will see it is too young and too afraid to fight."

"It will grow," said the Bear Catcher. "Six months ... a year..."

"And meantime it will have to be fed." The Master shook his head. "Not a penny over the odds," he said. "Take it or leave it."

"You strike a hard bargain," the Bear Catcher grumbled.

"And you bring me beasts I can do nothing with," the Master replied. "You should have left it to die in the forests of France and brought the mother only."

"You could teach it to dance," the Bear Catcher said.

"To dance?" The Master put back his head and laughed. "To dance, do you say?"

The Bear Catcher fingered the stubble on his chin.

"I've seen it done," he went on quietly. "With young ones. It's wonderful how a bed of hot coals will act on their feet. They'll lift them for that all right, as doubtless you or I would," and he lifted his own feet, one by one. The Master laughed again.

"Aye, aye, no doubt," he said. "And do you think I have time to teach a cub such tricks?"

"That boy of yours could manage it, I shouldn't wonder," the Bear Catcher said.

"What boy?" the Master frowned. "I have no boy here."

"The red-headed boy standing right behind you. The one who caught the cub a while back."

Dickon stiffened. Seemingly the Bear Catcher had eyes in the back of his head. Then, as the master swung round, he saw his chance and seized it.

"Your pardon, Master," he said, stepping forward. "The letter..."

"Letter?" the Master said, absently.

"From my master, the Tanner."

"Oh aye, the letter." But his bright, blue eyes were fixed intently on Dickon now as though seeing him for the first time. The Bear Catcher sidled closer.

"He has the gift," he said. "You saw how the beast ran to him. And when he touched it, it stayed still and didn't bite." The Master waved his hand to silence him.

"Could you?" he asked, his eyes still on Dickon. "Could you tame the bear cub and teach it to dance?"

"I...?"

"You." He nodded, his gaze unwavering. "Bear Catcher thinks you could."

Dickon swallowed, and looked from one to the other of them, seeing the Bear Catcher smile again, his small eyes as cold as pebbles. He shook his head. None of this had anything to do with him ... he had come with a letter, that was all.

"Not I," he said. "I know nothing of bears."

"And yet, 'tis true, the beast was still when you touched it," the Master said, stroking his beard thoughtfully. "A fluke, maybe?"

"One way to find out," the Bear Catcher said slyly. "Once let him go and you may never know."

"There's truth in that," the Master nodded. And then, suddenly making up his mind. "Try now," he said. Dickon shook his head, starting to back away. "Try now," the Master said again, catching him by the arm. "Approach the beast again. Then we shall see."

"But the letter..."

"Presently. As soon as you have shown me what you can do. Approach the beast ... if it does not bite or snap, then perhaps we may make a bargain."

Dickon looked across at the cub. It was squealing now and he could see that in its frantic efforts to escape it had twisted the rope that tethered it to the wagon wheel until it was tight around its neck, and now, half throttled, it still turned this way and that, scrabbling its claws against the earth while a little way off several of the men stood, laughing. The sight was so sad and pitiful that Dickon's heart went out to it.

"It will surely choke to death like that," he muttered, and shaking the Master's hand from his shoulder he walked slowly towards the wagon.

But this time when he came near, the cub only grew more desperate, redoubling its efforts. Dickon stood for a moment or two, watching it and puzzling what best to do. Young though it was, its claws were powerful enough to give him a nasty wound, and fear and pain might make it lash out.

"Well, boy, what now?" the Master shouted. "Afeard after all, are you?" Dickon could hear the men laughing. Much they would care if the poor beast clawed him to death, he thought. Or the Master either. He brushed a buzzing fly away from his face and squatted down beside the cub.

"Stop that," he told it crossly. "Stop now, and I'll untwist the rope ... just hold still."

At the sound of Dickon's voice the cub ceased its scrabbling, and giving a kind of squealing moan was suddenly still. In that instant Dickon grabbed the rope and unwound it from round the creature's throat, still talking as he did so.

"There now," he said, soft and low, and whistling between his teeth the while, the way Jacob used to when he groomed the grey mare. "That's a deal better, isn't it? All that struggling didn't help, you see... Only made things worse ... and they're bad

45

enough, I'd say." Slowly he reached out his hand and began to ease the rope, stretching it away from the cub's throat. To begin with it tossed about a bit, and once Dickon had to move his hand fast to avoid one of the paws. Then, breathing easily again, the cub sagged on to its haunches and went still. "Not so bad now, you see," Dickon said. And went on whistling. The cub was quiet now. It looked up at him, and began sniffing the air with little tosses of its head.

Then, swiftly, hungrily, it was reaching for his hand. At first Dickon tried to draw away from the curious, questing snout. But something told him the cub meant him no harm. Then he remembered, and grinned. Salt... Jacob had given his father's mare salt to lick for a treat. Maybe bears liked the stuff too. He must reek of it, working in the tannery as he did. Gently the cub began to lick his hand, until, satisfied, it gave a shuddering sigh and rested against his leg.

Another moment and it might have fallen asleep. Already its eyes were beginning to close. And then, suddenly, its head snapped up and Dickon heard footsteps behind him.

"Steady now, steady," he said quietly as it began to growl. "No danger while I'm by you, is there?"

The Master had taken a step backwards, seeing the cub's teeth laid bare. He cleared his throat.

"Seems Bear Catcher is right," he said. "How do you do it, lad?"

Dickon stood up and wiped his hands on his tunic. He didn't know how he did it, only that he felt sorry for the cub.

"It's a rare gift, right enough," the Bear Catcher said, coming up behind them, and Dickon saw him give the Master a crafty look. "A rare gift, indeed, and one that might be turned to your advantage, Master."

"Possibly, possibly," the Master said, looking at Dickon. "What's your name, lad?"

"Dickon."

"And you work for Master Nashe, the Tanner?"

"Yes, Master." Dickon frowned. The morning must be more than half over. "Your pardon, but the letter ... my master needs an answer."

"Aye, aye, you shall have your answer directly. I have not forgot the letter," the Master said, and putting his arm around Dickon's shoulder he began walking him towards the gate. "The matter stands like this," he said quietly, as soon as they were a little distance from the Bear Catcher, "if you could tame the bear cub, I've a mind to keep it." Dickon's heart began to beat fast, and he stared at the ground. "The beast is too small for the baiting," the Master went on, "but if it were tamed, taught to do some tricks maybe, I could use it to go through the streets before a baiting is to be put on, to let the people know." They had reached the gate by then, and the Master stopped, looking down at Dickon and stroking his beard. "The cub might be tamed..." he murmured after a moment. "What think you?"

"But I am apprentice to Master Nashe the Tanner," Dickon stammered. "Even if I could tame the cub, how could I serve two masters?"

"Aye, aye," the Master nodded, and went on stroking his beard. "There might be silver in this all the same," he went on after a moment "And it would be a pity to feed the creature to the dogs."

"To the dogs?" Dickon gasped.

The Master shrugged.

"What else would you have me do? 'Tis no use to me, being so young, as I told you."

Too young to be killed like that, Dickon thought, turning to look once more at the cub ... his cub, a pathetic bundle of brown fur that sat, watching him, its head to one side. He must do something ... but what? His mind raced.

"A pity," the Master said. "But there we are. You

are apprenticed to Master Nashe, as you say. And your master, the Tanner, has sent a letter asking when I shall have a bear hide for him, no doubt."

He had pulled the letter out of his pocket by then and was reading it through. Already, Dickon thought, it was too late. He looked at the cub again and swallowed. His throat felt tight and dry, and his heart was pounding. There must be a way to save the cub. But how?

Then, quite suddenly, the idea slipped into his mind.

"Sunday," he cried out, seizing the Master's arm. "I could come on Sunday. Will you keep the cub until then?"

Chapter Four

*T*he brightness has gone from the skies now. It is dark in this place and the smell is the smell of blood. The big bears roar in pain and fear, and all the birdsong has fled from the world. When the beasts with two legs come with their whips I crouch in the corner and try to hide. They point at me and mutter in a language I cannot understand. I look for the little beast with two legs, the gentle one, but he is not with them. Perhaps he will not come again.

If it is black dark outside, that is best. In the black dark time the beasts with two legs are asleep, the dogs in their kennels are quiet, and we are left alone. In the black dark time my mother speaks to me from the place where she is chained. She tells of the mountainside and the rushing streams, of the fish that leap in the streams and the birds that sing in the trees. And in that time I lift my head, sniffing for the wind that blows from the south, from the mountains where I was born.

Time, which had passed slowly enough for Dickon before that day, seemed now to move at the pace of the slowest snail, as he counted the hours until Sunday noon when he could return to the Bear Garden. The thought of the bear cub was never far from his mind as Thursday turned to Friday and Friday, at last, to Saturday. At night, before he went to sleep, he would remember the feel of the cub's fur under his hand, the way it had leant against his leg, and the small, bright black eyes that had looked up into his face. Like a pain inside him was the thought that the men might whip it, and he not by to stop them. Worse even than that, the worst of all, was the dread that the Master might change his mind. He had promised to keep the cub until Sunday, but would he keep his word? A hundred times a day Dickon seemed to hear the baying of the hounds; a hundred times a day he pushed the thought away. He must see the cub again. He must.

Now, instead of sleeping through the bell, he was awake before it rang, and first down to the pump, instead of last.

"There's a change going on here," Mistress Nashe muttered darkly, as she pushed him under the spout of cold water on the second day. " 'Tis the Southwark Fair your mind is running on, no doubt, and how fast you can get off to it, eh, Carrot Head?"

Dickon said nothing, letting her think what she pleased. He knew well enough that the Fair was to start on Monday. Ned had been talking of little else for the past two weeks, counting his money each evening and telling Dickon of all the sweetmeats he planned to buy. But the Fair meant little to Dickon. His thoughts were fixed on Sunday and would not stretch as far as Monday. On Sunday he would see the cub again. Nothing else mattered. Master Nashe had seemed well pleased with the answer Dickon had brought back from the Bear Garden, but Dickon knew that if he, or worse still Mistress Nashe, were to find out about the cub, it would put an end to all his hopes and plans. Many times he wished that Ann was close at hand, that he might tell her his secret, for she of all people would understand, but that would have to wait until Sunday, too, when he met her after the noonday dinner.

So Dickon hugged his secret to himself and counted the hours until he could see the cub again.

"Tomorrow," he thought, as he took out the fouled straw that Saturday morning. "Tomorrow I shall see the bear cub ... my bear cub."

When it was time for the short midday dinner

break Dickon left the others playing at dice in the yard and slipped into the stable, hoping to be alone. But Ned, seeing him go, followed him in there still babbling about the Southwark Fair.

"Master Nashe will give us time off," he said, squatting down beside Dickon. "A day and a half, I shouldn't wonder. You'll come with me, won't you? It will be grand, you'll see; there are jugglers and tumblers in the streets, and stalls with gingerbread, things to buy and all manner of folk to watch. And there will be plays at all the theatres, and bear baiting at the gardens by the river."

Dickon frowned, tossing his five stones from hand to hand, and then spreading them out on the ground in front of him. He wished Ned would go away. He wanted time on his own to think. Then, realizing that it had grown suddenly quiet, he looked up. Ned was watching him.

"What ails you?" he asked, leaning towards Dickon. "Don't you care about the Fair?"

"Of course I do," Dickon said.

"You've said nothing," Ned went on. "And you're different..." He frowned, trying to work it out. "Like you've got something on your mind, ever since Master Nashe sent you on that errand..."

Dickon's heart gave a lurch.

"I'm just the same as ever I was," he cut in. "Come on, I'll give you a game of fives if you like."

But Ned shook his head obstinately.

"No, you're not," he said. "Something happened, didn't it ... that day ... wherever it was the master sent you."

"Nothing happened," Dickon said, roughly. "That's just your fancy." And then, seeing Ned's eyes still on him, "If you must know, it's Mistress Nashe. She's forever scolding and finding fault, no matter what I do. If she has her way I shan't get to the Fair, so there's no use thinking about it."

"Of course you will," Ned said, the suspicion gone from his face at last. "All the 'prentices get a holiday when the Fair is on, that's the rule. Anyway," he went on, "it's the master who decides, not her."

"If it's like Bartholomew Fair, then I would like to go," Dickon said after a moment. "I went to that with my father. They had juggling there, and tumbling, and gingerbread stalls."

"I wager you've never seen a baiting, though, have you?" Ned cut in triumphantly. "Have you?" Dickon shook his head. "We're not really supposed to go," Ned went on, moving closer and lowering his voice. "But I know a way." His eyes were shining.

"'Tis grand sport I promise you, watching the dogs tearing those great ugly brutes to pieces."

Dickon thought of his bear cub and turned away from Ned's eager look.

"I doubt I'll have money for that," he muttered, rattling the five stones in his hand. "Look, do you want to play or not? They'll be calling us back to work soon."

For the moment Ned seemed satisfied, but it had been a near thing, Dickon thought. He would have to be more careful.

Wakening as the first sunlight crept through the attic window on Sunday morning, Dickon wondered how he could bear the slow passage of the hours until one o'clock when he would be free.

Master Nashe kept a strict house, and each Sunday led all his apprentices to church, dressed in their Sunday best, while Mistress Nashe stayed behind to prepare the midday dinner. Generally Dickon liked sitting in the cool dark of the church where the stained glass windows glowed like jewels when the sun shone through them. He liked the music, too, and always joined in the singing of the psalms, his voice rising pure and true. But not even the music could hold his attention that morning, and as the parson's sermon droned on and on, Dickon fidgeted and shuffled on the bench, until a sharp dig in the ribs and a glare from Master Nashe warned him he had better keep still.

But at last the service was over, the roast pork and pease pudding all eaten, his duties at table finished, and the bell tolling for one o'clock. It was the signal for them to go, and as Master Nashe pushed back his chair, belching contentedly, and waved his hand to dismiss them, Dickon was off the bench and first through the door into the yard.

As he raced towards the gate he could hear Ned calling to him, but nothing could stop him then.

At the corner of the street Ann was waiting for him as usual.

"Dickon," she gasped, as he flung his arms round her, none too gently. "Dickon ... what's this?" And then, pushing him away as soon as she was able to, she gazed intently into his face. "Something has happened, hasn't it?"

"Come on," he told her. "I'll show you."

"But where are we going?" Ann asked, for by then he had grabbed her arm and was pulling her unceremoniously along the street. "Dickon ... wait. I can't run as fast as you, just tell me."

"I'll tell you when we get to the churchyard," he said. They would be well away from the tannery by then and there would be no fear of Ned following them there. "Did you bring the Sunday cakes?"

"Of course," said Ann. "I always do."

Not until he started to tell Ann what had happened did he realize just how much the secret had weighed on him, and as the words came pouring out he had no doubt that she would understand. She always did. He began from the moment when Master Nashe had called him into the clerk's office and told him to write the letter, and there was a look of pride in her eyes at that. But later, when Dickon reached the part about the Bear Garden, and how the cub had run to him and the bargain he had made with the Master, she frowned, and turning her head away began to pluck at the grass where they were sitting, until at last Dickon's words faltered and died away. There was a feeling of sickness in the pit of his stomach as he stared at her.

"I thought you'd understand," he said.

"Dickon, Dickon dear." She looked intently at him and laid her hand on his arm. "This cannot be. The bear cub ... how will you be able to train it to dance?"

"I've thought of that," Dickon said. "I shall play

music for it." He pulled his flute from inside his jerkin. "See . . . it will dance when it hears the music. I know it will."

Ann shook her head.

"This is mere childishness," she said gently. "It is a wild animal. It knows nothing of music."

"It will work," Dickon said fiercely, shaking her hand from his arm. "I know it will."

Ann sighed. "And if it does, what then?"

"Then I will have saved its life," he said.

"And for what?" Ann asked, her gaze steady. "To go through the streets and lift its feet to a tune? To live like that until it grows large enough to be led into the ring and baited like the others?" Dickon frowned. "Besides," Ann went on, "you cannot serve two masters. Once Master Nashe discovers – "

"But he won't," Dickon flashed. "At least come with me, Ann. Then you'll see for yourself."

"To the Bear Garden?" A look of alarm flitted across her face.

"Please," Dickon begged. "Please. I want you to see the bear cub . . . you'll understand then."

"I understand now," Ann said. "And you should not ask me to go to such a fearful place. You should not go yourself."

"Not go?" Dickon stared at her.

"I speak for your own good," Ann said.

Dickon felt a flush begin to creep over his face.

"It was for my own good that my mother and stepfather took me out of school and sent me as an apprentice to Master Nashe," he said, his voice rising angrily. "Now you speak in the same way."

"Dickon," Ann whispered, her eyes suddenly filling with tears. "Oh, Dickon, how could you?"

He didn't care. His cheeks were burning as he faced her.

"I thought you'd understand," he shouted. "You of all people, that's what I told myself. But you care no more than they did. Well, I know better about my own good than you do, and if you will not come with me then I will go by myself."

For a moment there was silence. Then Ann brushed the tears away with the back of her hand.

"Go then," she said in a low voice. "Go and see your bear cub, since you know so much better than I do. And take the cakes with you."

"All right, I will," he said, snatching at the bundle in her lap and meaning to leave her there. But Ann caught his wrist and held him fast.

"Does it mean so much?" she asked. "I've never seen you like this before. Does it, Dickon?" The anger left him then as suddenly as it had come, and he nodded emptily. "But why?"

"Because it is something I can do," he said after a moment. "And because..." he frowned, searching for the words, "because the cub trusted me. It came to me. ME. I am the only one who can save its life. Don't you understand that?"

Ann nodded slowly.

"But I am afraid for you," she said. "Afraid of what might happen... Oh, if only Father were still alive!"

"I think that often," Dickon muttered. "But it does no good."

"I know." She sighed. "Poor Dickon ... you hate it at the tannery, don't you?"

"More than you can ever know," he told her.

"You and that poor bear cub have much in common, I'm thinking. Both of you are prisoners in a way."

Just then the bell tolled the half hour. Dickon looked towards the gate. Already thirty precious minutes had slipped past. Ann gave a sigh.

"You had better go then, since your heart is set on it," she said. But for a moment he didn't move. Ann watched him.

"You'll say nothing, will you?" he blurted out at

last. "It must be a secret, Ann. If you tell our mother
– " She shook her head.

"I will tell her nothing," she said. "I promise . . .
only Dickon, you must send me word."

"But you know I cannot leave the tannery." He
frowned.

"I will find a way," Ann said. "Now go, and take
the cakes with you."

He turned at the lych-gate and waved to her. She
was still sitting on the grass where he had left her,
her hands in her lap.

And then he was off, running along Bankside
towards the Bear Garden.

*Today the little beast with two legs has come to the dark
place. I know him by his smell and because he is all
gentleness. He has a stick with him, but it is not for
hitting with. When he puts it to his mouth it makes a
good sound. The sound is like water running over stones,
like wind in the trees, like the song of birds. I go close to
the little beast and listen. I smell the good smell on his
hands, and when he touches me I am not afraid.
Although he is little he is stronger than I am for he
unbinds the straps that are tight around my nose. Then
he gives me a new food to eat. It is good to taste.*

He makes a sound. "Sit. Sit." Again and again he

makes the sound. I do not know what it means, but when I go down on my haunches he is pleased and gives me more of the good thing to eat. If I go down on my haunches when he makes the sound I get a piece of the good thing. One of the big beasts with two legs watches us. After a long while the little beast with two legs goes away. Then they put the straps back on my nose.

But the smell of the little beast stays on me where he has touched my fur. It is a good smell, and I curl up on the straw and sleep.

Chapter Five

The sun was dipping down behind the roofs on Bankside when Dickon left the Bear Garden, and set off at a run across the bean field. Already he had stayed longer than he should have done. In an hour, maybe two, it would be dusk and time for the curfew bell to sound. He must be back at the tannery in good time. Now, more than ever, no one must suspect where he had been.

For the cub had known him. It had eaten from his hand, and when he played music on his flute he had watched it grow still, listening intently. It had even sat at his command. Dickon could hardly believe it himself when the bear cub had gone down on its haunches, not once but twice, and the Master, watching from a little way off, had nodded his approval, urging him on and murmuring to Osric who stood near at hand that he'd never seen the like of it. After that there had been no more talk of feeding the cub to the hounds. Instead, when it was time to go, the Master had put an arm round Dickon's shoulder and told him to come again at the same time next week.

"'Tis a pity we could not have had it trained up for the Southwark Fair," he said. "But by Christmas perhaps ... how say you, Osric?"

"Mebbe," Osric shrugged. "Best ask your young wizard here. He seems to have a way with the beast." And he cast a sour look in Dickon's direction.

"Well, we'll see," the Master said. And Dickon, thinking of all the Sundays that were to come for the next three months, forgot about Osric as the Master walked him towards the gate. In the golden glow of the setting sun all the world seemed brighter, and he knew that he had been right not to listen to Ann.

Turning into the alleyway where, just three days before, he had first seen the Bear Catcher, Dickon's mind was still on the cub, so that he didn't see the hooded figure waiting in the shadows until it was too late. There was a quick movement, and a hand shot out and gripped him.

"Let go," he gasped, wriggling and squirming in the iron grasp, and cursing himself for not being more watchful. "Let go ... if it's money you're after I have none."

"You take me for a cutpurse, do you?" a voice said, with a kind of chuckle that Dickon remembered well, and with his free hand the man pushed the hood back from his head. A wave of relief swept over Dickon.

"Jacob!" he gasped.

"So – you recognize me now, do you?" he grinned.

"You gave me a fright," Dickon said, "jumping out at me like that. But I'm mighty glad to see you just the same."

"And I you, lad," he nodded, peering into Dickon's face. "Come, let's get into the light. Then I can take a closer look at you." And hurrying Dickon along the alley and out on to Bankside, he held him at arm's length and looked him up and down. "You've grown a fair measure since I last saw you. And things is different now, eh? But you've not forgotten your old Jacob?"

"That I never would," Dickon told him. "But how came you to be here?"

"Ah now." Jacob put his head on one side and tapped his nose with his forefinger. "Now there's a tale ... I was sent for by a little bird ... the sweetest little bird – "

"Ann," Dickon said.

"Your sweet sister, aye, and I was just on my way to the Bear Garden to find you, when along you come, full pelt, head in the clouds as usual."

"You knew where I'd be?" Dickon frowned. "Ann told you?"

"She touched upon the matter, aye," Jacob nodded, his eyes on Dickon's face. "Something about a bear cub, from what I could understand."

"You know that, too," Dickon muttered, drawing back with a frown. "And after she promised – "

"Promised not to tell your lady mother," Jacob cut in swiftly, catching him by the shoulders. "Never said anything about not telling me, now did she?"

It was true, Dickon thought, remembering Ann's words in the churchyard. She must have made up her mind then and there to send Jacob to find him.

"I'd rather you knew than anyone," he said at last.

"That's better," Jacob nodded. "You can trust old Jacob, you know that. Close as an oyster, that's me." And he tapped the side of his nose again, head on one side, and grinned.

"Ann wouldn't come," Dickon said. "She was afraid, I think." Jacob nodded. "But you're here ... and... Oh, Jacob, I'm glad. You'll help me, won't you? That would be a fine thing. I wish you'd been here sooner, I have to get back to the tannery now, or

I'll be in trouble. But if you could only see the cub ... the way it trusts me. Today I taught it to sit. And..."

But Jacob had started to whistle under his breath, the way he used to when he groomed the grey mare in the stable, and didn't seem to be listening. Dickon stopped.

"What is it?" he frowned. "Don't you want to help me?"

"Help you to see sense, maybe," Jacob said, rubbing a grimy hand over his bald head. "Help you to get out of the peck of trouble you're landing yourself in – worrying your sweet sister to death."

"They would have killed it," Dickon cut in. "Don't you understand? They would have thrown it to the dogs."

"Beasts are dying every day," Jacob said with a shrug. "What makes your precious cub so different, tell me that?"

"Because it IS mine," Dickon cried. "You said it yourself. 'Your precious cub', that's what you said. And because I can save it."

Jacob grunted. "For the moment, maybe," he said. "But for how long? And what will you do if things turn nasty?"

"The Master has promised –"

"Aye, I warrant he has," Jacob cut in. "The Master of the Bear Garden will promise anything if it's to his advantage. But he's not the only one, is he? There's some in that place as I'd not trust as far as I could throw them with my hands bound behind my back. And here's another thing ... what when your master at the tannery gets wind of all this. What say you to that, young master? It'll be out of the frying pan into the fire then, I fancy?"

Dickon kicked at the cobblestones, thinking of the cub sitting on the pile of straw where he had left it.

"Ann has put you up to this, hasn't she?" he said, looking up. "She wanted you to stop me going to the Bear Garden again, that's why you've come."

"Hush now, lad," Jacob muttered. "No need to take it so green over the bows." But Dickon brushed aside his outstretched hand.

"Well, it's no good," he said fiercely. "I won't be stopped ... not even by you. It's too important. Don't you see that?"

For a moment there was silence. Then, unexpectedly, Jacob's nut-brown face creased and crumpled and he began to chuckle.

"Same old Master Dickon," he said, rubbing his hand over his head once more. "Stubborn as any mule once you get an idea into your head. I told her,

I told your sweet sister, 'You'll not change his mind now,' I said. 'Not once he's set upon a thing.'"

Dickon took a deep breath and smiled.

"You may tell her you tried your best," he said.

"Aye," Jacob said with a nod, growing serious again. "Aye." He sighed. "'Tis a hard and dangerous course you've set yourself, young master. And there's heartbreak in it somewhere, I'm thinking."

But Dickon was impatient of more warnings, and the great bell on St Paul's was tolling the half hour.

"I must go," he said. "If I'm not back before curfew I shall get a beating. Will you come with me next Sunday, Jacob? You know the ways of animals better than I, you could help me. Besides, if Ann knows you're with me, 'twill make her less fearful." Jacob sucked in his breath slowly and looked at Dickon with his head on one side.

"Taught it to sit, did you?" he said at last.

Dickon grinned.

"Say you'll come," he said.

"Happen I may be around," Jacob nodded. "Aye, happen I may. Never far off if you need a friend," he went on after a moment. "You know that, don't you, young master?" Dickon nodded. "Send for me at the Globe, over yonder," he said, with a jerk of his head.

"Ann told me you were working there," Dickon

said. And then stood, not wanting to say goodbye.

"Off with you, then," Jacob told him. "Off with you ... unless you want that beating you told me of."

Dickon nodded once more. Then turned and ran.

It was only when he was through the churchyard and out into the street again that he remembered the Southwark Fair, which was to start the next morning. Already the preparations had begun. Booths were being set up on each side of the street, and there were horses and carts and goods being unloaded. Around London Bridge the crowd was so thick with people hurrying to get across before curfew that Dickon had much ado to push his way through. He would have liked to linger, but dared not, for fear that the bell would begin to toll before he could reach the tannery. Turning into Twill Lane itself he saw a company of tumblers, two men, a woman and a girl, all dark haired, their wagon bright with coloured ribbons. The girl laughed and waved as he stopped for a moment to watch them go past.

He was only just in time. Gilbert was already starting to close the heavy, barred gates.

"Here he is! Here comes the snail," he shouted over his shoulder as Dickon skidded past him and into the yard.

"Last – as usual," Mistress Nashe said, looking up

from the pot she was stirring. "The others have been back this half hour."

"I'm not late though, am I?" Dickon muttered, which might have cost him a cuff on the ear had not the curfew bell begun to sound at that moment.

Seeing that she was worsted, Mistress Nashe contented herself with giving Dickon a hard look.

"Get to the table, Carrot Head," she said spitefully, "and hold your tongue."

Dickon did as he was told, sliding on to the bench beside Ned and bowing his head meekly as Master Nashe said the grace. Sunday evenings were always a bleak time at the tannery, with the week stretching endlessly ahead. After the brightness of the afternoon it seemed worse than ever that evening. Even Ned was silent, hunched sullenly over his food and never once glancing in Dickon's direction. Later, when they were getting ready for bed, he sat on the stool with his back to Dickon, pulling off his shoes and stockings without a word. When Dickon asked him what was wrong he shook his head and wouldn't answer.

"Is it something I have done," Dickon frowned. "If so, I ask your pardon. But what is it?"

Ned turned round then, his mouth drawn down into a sulky line and gave him a hard stare.

"You could have waited for me," he said.

"Waited – ?" Dickon stared at him blankly.

"I called and called, but you ran off without a word. I wanted you to come with me and see the stalls being set up for the Southwark Fair."

Dickon bit his lip.

"I had to meet my sister," he said.

"You always have to meet your sister," Ned muttered, tugging off his shoe. "Anyway, where did you go all afternoon?" By the flickering light of the rush candle Dickon saw the look of suspicion in his eyes.

"Only to the churchyard," Dickon told him. "And a little way along Bankside. I'm sorry, Ned, in truth I am. She's lonely, you see, since my father died." Ned dropped his gaze, but his mouth stayed in a sulky line. "I'll come to the Fair with you, and gladly," Dickon went on, feeling suddenly guilty, for Ned had been a good friend to him since he arrived at the tannery, shielding him from trouble when he could.

No sooner were the words out than Dickon wished them unsaid. But it was too late. Already Ned's face had brightened a little.

"You will?" he asked. "You promise?"

"I promise," Dickon said.

"'Twill be a whole day that we get off," Ned whispered as soon as they were in bed and Gilbert had snuffed the candle. "I heard them talking, the master and mistress. He said he supposed they'd have to allow us that much, and she grumbled and said she supposed so."

Dickon's heart leapt suddenly. A whole day when he might be with the cub . . . except that he had promised Ned.

"Which day will it be?" he asked.

"Friday, maybe, or Saturday. We'll have a fine time, Dickon, you see if we don't," Ned told him. "We'll get money to spend, too."

"Quiet over there," Gilbert told them from the other bed. "We're trying to get to sleep."

"Your pardon, Gilbert," Ned replied. And turning over and rolling himself into a ball he was soon snoring.

But Dickon lay awake for some time, staring into the darkness and wondering what he was going to do. A whole, precious day of freedom when he might have been with the cub. And he had given it up to Ned. I'm caught in a snare of my own making, he thought, and now I don't know how to get out of it.

For the next two days Ned kept nudging him and winking, as though they shared some secret. Once he whispered in Dickon's ear that he must let him choose what they were to do on their free day. Dickon merely nodded and went on with his sweeping. It would be all the same to him, he thought, since he couldn't go to the Bear Garden. Anyway, Dickon was not sure even now that Master Nashe meant to give them a day off. The work at the tannery went on as usual, and by the time Wednesday morning came, nothing had been said.

"He keeps us dangling, like fish on a hook," Ned told Dickon while they played at five stones during the midday dinner hour. Outside, beyond the high, brick wall they could hear all the hubbub of the fair in full swing, but that week the gates, which were usually kept open from first light until nightfall, were closed to the outside world, and Master Nashe kept the apprentices hard at work.

"I don't believe he means to give us time off at all," Dickon said.

But Ned shook his head.

"'Tis the rule," he said. "Gilbert told me. Like Christmas and Saints' Days. You'll see, 'twill be Friday or Saturday for sure."

But another day passed and still Master Nashe said nothing.

It wasn't until Thursday evening at supper that he

pronounced Saturday would be a holiday and there would be no work at the tannery on that day. Then, pulling a small leather purse from his pocket and pouring some coins from it on to the table in front of him, he said he supposed they had all better have something to spend at the Fair. Mistress Nashe looked on, her blue eyes bulging with disapproval.

"You're never going to give HIM something as well," she snapped when it came to Dickon's turn. "That snail, that Carrot Head, who is always late and has hardly earned his keep these three months."

Dickon felt the anger well up inside him. He had worked as hard as the others and had done everything he was told. He had been the first at the pump for the past six days, and still she tormented him. He turned on the bench and looked Mistress Nashe straight in the face. It was a look, no more, but Mistress Nashe gave a gasp.

"There's a devil in that boy," she cried, pointing a quivering finger at him. "Do you see, husband? Do you see the insolent look he gives me? Oh, let me get at the broom, I'll beat him till he's black and blue."

"Hold your peace, wife," Master Nashe thundered, suddenly crashing his fist on the table so that the coins jumped and rattled. "I find no fault with the lad, and if he has a devil in him, as you say, I think you may leave it to me to beat it out of him."

Mistress Nashe opened her mouth. Then closed it again, and for long moment there was silence. At last, casting a venomous look at Dickon she rose from her place and marched from the room.

Master Nashe cleared his throat.

"Five groats," he said, pushing the coins towards Dickon. The two older boys were shuffling their feet. Ned nudged Dickon in the ribs and smirked. But Dickon, clutching the coins in his hand, said not a word. He had won, but he felt no triumph. Only from that moment, something had changed. He knew that from then on Mistress Nashe would hate him more than ever.

The next afternoon Master Nashe beckoned him over when work was finished for the day.

"Three months since you came to the tannery," he rumbled, pulling at his moustache.

"Yes, Master," Dickon said.

"Time to start work in earnest. On Monday you begin with the knife."

It was what Dickon had dreaded most. Now that it had come, there was nothing he could do. He glanced at the beam that ran across the ceiling. It was empty that afternoon, all had been cleared away for the end of the week. But by Monday there would be pigs, sheep, a cow maybe; worst of all, there might be a bear. He closed his eyes and swallowed.

"Yes, Master," he said.

Chapter Six

The sun was well up when Mistress Nashe rang the bell the following morning, and breakfast half over before the master himself appeared to take his place at the table. There would be no more work done in the tannery until Monday, and for once no one was in a hurry. A whole day of freedom stretched ahead.

Dickon, thinking of his bear cub and of how he might have a chance to see it that day, listened with only half an ear to Master Nashe's rumbled warnings about thieves and cutpurses, about not getting into fights or arguments with other apprentices and how they must all be back by curfew or woe betide them. The five groats were safely in his pocket; he would buy something for the cub, he thought. And before leaving the attic that morning he had taken his flute from the chest and, re-rolling it carefully in the piece of old blue cloth that he kept wrapped around it, he had thrust it deep inside his tunic. As for Monday, he pushed that thought to the back of his mind. A whole day of freedom stretched ahead, the sky was fair and bright, and somehow, later on maybe, he would find a way to give Ned the slip and see the cub.

"Away with you, then," Master Nashe nodded, his warnings finally ended. Peter and Gilbert were gone in a moment, and Ned, catching hold of Dickon's arm, pulled him across the yard and through the gates.

"Now for the Fair," he cried, his sallow face flushed with excitement. "Mind, Dickon, you've given your word to do whatever I want today. Remember that."

"I remember," Dickon said.

"Say it, say you promise."

"All right, then," Dickon nodded. "I promise."

Ned grinned, and linked his arm through Dickon's.

"I wanted to surprise you," he said. "I thought you'd make some excuse not to go there, but now you've promised it's all right."

"Go where?" Dickon asked.

"Can't you guess?" Ned asked, giving him a sidelong look. "To the Bear Garden, that's where, to see the bears fight. 'Twill be grand sport there today, I warrant you."

Too late Dickon saw what a fool he had been not to guess where Ned meant to go. All the things he had been saying, for the past week or more . . . it had been plain enough, if only he had listened. And now he had promised all over again, and there was no way out.

At first he tried to hold Ned back, dawdling by the gingerbread stall where the warm, sweet smell of freshly baked cakes wafted out towards them. But Ned caught him roughly by the arm and would have none of it.

"If the baiting starts before we get there 'twill be too late to get in," he told him.

"Perhaps they'll not let us in anyway," Dickon said. "The other day you told me we're not supposed to go. Besides, I only have five groats. That's not enough, is it?"

But Ned gave him a wink.

"I know a way of getting in and having money left over," he said. Dickon didn't answer. Ned watched him for a moment. "Of course, if you're afeard to go. . ." he began, his eyes suddenly suspicious.

"Not I," Dickon cut in swiftly. "What is there to be afeard of?"

"Why, the bears, of course," Ned answered. "They're ugly brutes, you'll see. Great, shaggy brown devils. And fight..." His eyes gleamed. "Last time when I was there one of them slipped its chain and ran round the ring with the dogs at its heels."

"You mean it escaped?"

"Nah, they never escape. It put up a good fight before they caught it, though. And did for one of the dogs ... blood everywhere, there was ... worse than our tannery." He grinned. "Come on, we'd best run."

Dickon didn't want to run, he didn't want to get to the Bear Garden at all, not like this, not with Ned. As though looking through the wrong end of a spy glass he saw the booths that lined the streets. One had red apples and pears on it, another had onions, carrots and cabbages, and next to it a booth with lengths of cloth, ribbons and lace; chickens and ducks in crates, and pigs, squealing in a pen with a thin, tall woman peering down at them and arguing the price with the farmer. A maid was crying "Sweet Lavender," and a little further on a pedlar with a tray of remedies for sickness held up a bottle with some green liquid in it as they passed. And all the time Ned kept a tight hold of Dickon's arm, pushing past the groups of people who jostled and talked around them, while the Bear Garden grew closer and closer. The sky was pale blue, and as they turned down towards the river and came within sight of the great wooden building itself, Dickon wished himself a hundred miles away.

It wasn't just that he didn't want to see the bears fight. A new fear had taken hold of him. If any of the men at the Bear Garden should see him there and recognize him, then his secret would be out.

"Don't say a word, now," Ned was saying, his mouth close to Dickon's ear. "Just you leave this to me."

People were crowding towards the entrance to the Bear Pit. Already Dickon could make out the burly figure of the Master himself, waving them on and shouting that he had fine bears newly arrived from South Western France for fighting that day.

"I can't go on with this," Dickon thought. "Promise or no promise. I'll have to make a run for it."

And then, just as he had nerved himself to break free of Ned's grip, when they were within a few paces of the entrance so that Dickon was sure the Master must see him amongst the crowd and recognize him by his red hair, Ned gave a wink and, ducking out of the line of people, he doubled back around the side of the Bear Pit, dragging Dickon after him, until they reached a clump of hawthorn bushes. Then, looking once over his shoulder to make sure they hadn't been seen, Ned went down on his hands and knees and began to run his hand along the planks that formed the side of the building.

"What are you doing?" Dickon asked, relief at his narrow escape making his voice suddenly loud.

"Ssh," Ned warned him. "Do you want someone to find us?"

Dickon watched him.

" 'Twas here last year," Ned muttered "...unless they've mended it. I swear it was about here..." Then he gave a sudden grunt, and Dickon saw that one of the planks was loose. By easing the board to one side, Ned made a space just large enough to crawl through. "Told you we wouldn't have to pay, didn't I?" he grinned. Then, with a quick look over his shoulder, he caught hold of Dickon's arm and pulled him down until their faces were level. "You first," he said.

"But – "

"Unless you're afeard."

There was nothing for it. Belly down, Dickon began to wriggle through the gap.

Edging forward into the darkness he could smell the earth under his face, and from above came the trample and thump of feet as people climbed up to the rows of seats inside the Bear Pit. Then Ned was beside him.

"Reckon that's the last time I'll be able to get through that gap," he muttered. "Come on, I'll show you the way."

Dickon crawled after him through the thudding, creaking darkness. As his eyes became accustomed to the gloom he could see a patch of light just ahead. A moment later Ned had scrambled through into the Bear Pit and Dickon, close on his heels, found himself amongst a forest of petticoats and stockinged legs. Ned put out a hand and hauled him to his feet, and then, linking arms with him, began to squirm his way through the crowd of people towards the ring-side.

"Now we shall see something," he grinned triumphantly when at last they reached the wooden rail that ran around the ring.

Dickon gripped the rail, and turned to look at the great press of people who swayed and shuffled all around him, like a forest in the wind. Further back, above the heads of the groundlings who filled the space beside the ring, there were tiers of seats rising to the topmost rim of the great, round building, and above that the open sky.

He closed his eyes for a moment, smelling the scent of fresh sawdust which wafted up from beyond the rail. Then opened them again and stared at the heavy wooden post with iron hoops set into it that stood in the middle of the ring. He could see where they would bring the bears from. There was a gate mid-way around the ring, and beyond that a passage leading out to the back. Somewhere out there was his cub. Above the noise of the crowd he could hear the baying of the dogs.

The barking grew louder, and hearing the sound the crowd stirred, each person straining forward towards the ring. Dickon felt himself squeezed against the railing by a huge man in a red, feathered cap.

" 'Twill start soon now," he told the fat girl beside him, and putting his arm round her gave her a squeeze.

For an instant the crowd grew quiet, watching and waiting. Then they began to murmur; the murmuring grew to a mighty roar, and Dickon felt the ground begin to shake and tremble with the stamp of a hundred feet. Ned nudged him in the ribs, his eyes glowing with excitement as he pointed towards the passageway, and at that moment Dickon saw the Master himself come striding into the ring.

"Good people," he began, waving them to silence. "Good people, welcome all, welcome to the Bear Garden. Our bears are the fiercest in the world, their teeth will bite, their claws will tear..." here there was a roar of approval from the crowd, "...but our dogs are fierce, too, and you will see who is the victor and who the vanquished this day. Good people all, for your entertainment this day, we present first a great she-bear newly arrived from France."

Dickon felt his heart give a lurch, for it was his cub's dam, he was sure of it. But there was a stirring among the crowd, heads were shaken, and a shout went up around the Bear Pit.

"Harry Hunks," cried the big man behind Dickon, snatching the red-feathered cap from his head and waving it in the air. "We want Harry Hunks." The Master paused a moment.

"Good people all, we crave your patience," he smiled. "Later you shall see the great, the invincible HARRY HUNKS! First, the she-bear from France. I warrant you she'll give rare sport. You'll get your money's worth this day, for you know, good people, that woman kind make doughty fighters –" There was laughter then, and someone shouted:

"Show us the she-bear, then."

"Aye, aye," bellowed the crowd. "The she-bear. Bring on the she-bear."

The Master bowed and then, signalling towards the passageway with a wave of his hand, he stood aside and the next moment the huge, looming figure of the bear came into view, dragged by several men and roaring with fear and pain as they whipped her along.

"Now they will tie her up," Ned bellowed, grabbing Dickon's arm excitedly and pointing towards the post. "Then they will bring on the dogs..."

At first, as the pack of dogs circled round the poor, chained beast, Dickon thought he could bear it for a while longer if he gripped the rail tightly enough. Once or twice he closed his eyes, but Ned kept digging him in the ribs and yelling at him above the roar of the crowd, so he must needs watch even though the sight made him sick.

The dogs ran back and forth, making lunges at the bear's legs, until one, bolder than the rest, leapt at her back and shoulders. But the bear was too quick for it, and with one mighty swipe struck at the dog and laid it upon the sawdust at her feet where it gave one whimper, and then stayed still and did not move again. For a while the others kept their distance, barking and circling uncertainly around the bear. Then Dickon saw the gate opened and three more dogs ran into the ring, fiercer and stronger than the first ones, and the crowd howled with delight. Ned was waving his fist in the air.

" 'Tis a good bear," he yelled, turning to look at Dickon. "See how well she fights ... but this lot will have her down before long."

As he spoke, Dickon saw the bear turn her head this way and that. One huge hound had leapt at her back again, while two more attacked her from the other side. In vain she struck out with her claws. There were too many of them, and where one failed another succeeded. The blood began to flow from her head and ears in a slow trickle, and with a roar the bear tossed her head, half blinded now and trying to shake the crimson gouts from her eyes.

Dickon could watch no more. He had to get out ... now ... this minute, while Ned's eyes were still fixed on the ring. Turning away, he shoved desperately past the man with the red-feathered hat, and dived into the crowd, fighting and squirming his way past the tight packed bodies that filled the Bear Pit.

After what seemed a long time he was outside, leaning against the timbers and taking huge breaths of fresh air. His legs were shaking, and he felt a sob rise in his throat, so that he turned his face to the wall of the Bear Pit and banged his fist against the planks. But even with his eyes closed he couldn't shut out the sight of the wounded bear with her torn flesh and the blood running down her snout, or the glowing, cheering faces of the crowd. In a year, maybe two, when it was full grown, it could be his bear cub chained to the post baited and tortured by a pack of hounds as the mob howled with pleasure.

"Never," he muttered fiercely. "Never, never... I would do anything to stop that." And brushing the helpless, angry tears from his eyes he straightened up.

Just in front of him a girl was doing cartwheels on the grass. He frowned, rubbing his sleeve across his face again. Somewhere he had seen her before. She stopped for a moment to catch her breath and, looking across at Dickon, smiled at him. He remembered then. She was the girl he had seen on the cart with the company of tumblers on Sunday.

"You come out," she said shyly. "You don't like to see bears fight?"

"No," Dickon muttered. "It's cruel ... horrible."

"I think, too," she nodded, in quick agreement.

"Do you?" Dickon asked awkwardly. "Truly?"

She nodded again, and for a moment sadness clouded her face as she glanced towards the Bear Pit where a great roar had gone up. Then someone called to her, and looking across the grass Dickon saw the tumbler's booth set up a little distance away. She waved back at the man who stood there, and then, smiling once more at Dickon, ran off.

Suddenly Dickon's mind was clear. What he wanted now was to be with his cub. He looked quickly round, but there was no sign of Ned; probably, Dickon thought, he hadn't even noticed that he had gone. Later, when they were back at the tannery, Dickon thought, he would tell him that he had had the stomach ache and that was why he had gone outside. He took a deep breath and, stopping only to pick up a half-eaten apple that someone had thrown on to the grass, he started to run towards the gate at the back of the Bear Pit.

The wicket was fastened that day, but as the Master himself had told Dickon to come whenever he wished, he vaulted over it and stood looking round the yard.

He could see Osric and Slim amongst the men gathered around the back entrance of the pit. For a moment Dickon frowned, remembering the way Osric had looked at him on Sunday, casting a sudden shadow over the brightness of the afternoon. But Osric was too busy to notice him today and, without waiting any longer, Dickon skirted the sunlit yard and pushed open the door to the outhouse where the cub was kept.

Once inside, he stood with his back against the door until his eyes had grown accustomed to the gloom and he could see the bars of the cage and the shadowy outline of the hay loft above it. There was a rustle, and a low whimpering sound, and as Dickon moved forward he could make out the darker outline of the cub lying on the straw at the far end of the stall. Kneeling down beside the bars he gave a low whistle.

At first the cub didn't move. Dickon whistled again, and this time he saw it lift its head, snuffing the air. He reached inside his jerkin for the apple.

"Look what I've brought you," he murmured softly. "Come now ... come here and see."

At the sound of his voice the cub stood up and started to move towards him. Dickon could hear the clink of the chain dragging along the ground as it came. There was no need to tether it to the wall like that, he thought, frowning. The poor beast couldn't escape from a locked cage. As it came closer it started to snuffle and push its nose towards the bars.

"Not forgotten me, then?" Dickon said, putting out his hand to stroke its head. " 'Tis nearly a week since I saw you." He broke off a piece of the apple and held it through the bars. The cub tried to take it, but it couldn't get its jaws far enough apart for the leather muzzle that was fixed over its head and snout.

"This won't do," Dickon muttered. "Here, let's try and get you free of the pesky thing." And stretching his arms through the bars he began to feel around for the buckle. The cub, not understanding, plunged and strained away from him, pushing with its back legs, and then sitting down on the ground and lifting one of its front paws to try and push him away. "Hold still, can't you," Dickon told it, struggling with the buckle. "I'm doing my best." With a final tug he pulled the muzzle free of the cub's snout.

So intent was he, that he hadn't heard the sound of soft footsteps outside. Not until the door creaked open did Dickon swing round, pulling his arms hastily back through the bars.

Ned was standing in the doorway, grinning at him.

"You're a fine one, then," he said. "Thought you could give me the slip, I suppose."

Dickon stood up.

"You followed me," he said. Ned nodded, slowly, licking his lips.

"I knew all along you were up to something," he said. "Stuck out a mile." His gaze wandered towards the cage. "What you got in there, anyway?"

Dickon looked at him. It was too late to lie, now. Maybe if he could get Ned on his side...

"It's a bear cub," he said.

Ned stared at him in disbelief. Then a slow, stupid smile spread over his face.

"Puppy dog, more like," he said. "A nice little puppy dog. You were afeard in there, weren't you?" he went on. "I know. That's why you ran off..."

Dickon shook his head.

"I didn't want to watch any more," he said quietly. "That's all. It was horrible ... the most horrible thing I've ever seen. And I wanted to be here with the cub, that's why I left."

"Liar," Ned retorted. "You're even afeard of the dead animals in the workshop. I've seen the way you look at them. So what have you got in there?"

"See for yourself," Dickon shrugged.

Ned had held fast to the door until then, as though ready to take to his heels if need be. Now curiosity got the better of him and he edged forward.

"Slowly now," Dickon told him. "It doesn't know you yet. It may be afraid."

Already the cub had moved back to its pile of straw and was crouched there, watching with its head lowered.

"And I suppose you're its best friend?" Ned sneered. "This bear cub you're pretending you've got." And bounding suddenly forward he grasped the bars and stared into the cage.

The cub, frightened by the sudden movement, lowered its head and, swaying a little from side to side, growled menacingly. Ned's face turned a pasty white, and he let go of the bars.

"I told you," Dickon said.

"Ugly brute," Ned muttered, backing away. "What does it want to do that for? It didn't growl at you."

"That's because it trusts me," Dickon said. "Look, stay there and I'll show you." And crouching down beside the bars he started to coax the cub out of its corner, whistling the tune it liked and holding out a piece of the apple again. It came slowly this time, one eye still on Ned, until it was sitting near enough for Dickon to be able to stretch through the bars and stroke its head. "You see..." Dickon said, turning to look over his shoulder.

But Ned didn't answer. His jaw sagged, and he took a step backwards, staring at Dickon and shaking his head.

Dickon frowned. He had seen that look before. That was the way the men had stared at him the first day he came to the Bear Garden, when the cub had run to him. He pushed the thought away.

"It's only that it trusts me," he said.

But Ned was edging towards the door.

"I'm not staying here," he muttered. "'Tis unnatural, that's what it is. Or worse ... making friends with a wild beast like that." He jerked his head towards the cub. "'Tis some kind of sorcery, I'd say."

Sorcery. The word burned itself into Dickon's mind. Looking up at Ned's face he saw that he was in danger. He must try to make him understand. If he couldn't do that, his secret would be out, and there would be no hope for the cub. He sprang to his feet.

"Listen," he said urgently. "Listen, please, Ned. That day, the day Master Nashe sent me on an errand, it was here, to the Bear Garden. The Bear Catcher had newly come from France, and the cub escaped and ran to me. I can't tell why ... it just did." He saw Ned's eyes flicker and turn away. "I was there," he went on, "that was all ... and it came and stopped at my feet. I didn't whip it or harm it, just petted it a little, like you would a cat or a dog. And now it trusts me ... can't you understand?"

But Ned's face was a blank. He wasn't listening.

" 'Tis the devil's work you do here," he said, his voice thin and high. "Mistress Nashe was right about you all along, I'm thinking. 'Tis unnatural. Wait till they hear of this."

"No!" Dickon cried. "You mustn't tell them. You mustn't tell anyone."

He sprang to his feet. The cub, sensing that something was amiss had begun to growl again. Suddenly it rose up on its hind legs, and Dickon saw Ned's eyes widen in fear. He started to back towards the door.

"Wait!" Dickon said desperately. "Ned, wait. There's no need to be afraid."

He went towards him.

"Don't touch me!" Ned hissed.

Then, from outside, came the sound of voices, and of something heavy being dragged along the ground. Ned licked his lips, and darted a glance over his shoulder. For a moment he stood as though frozen. The next instant he had flung himself at the door and was through it before Dickon could stop him.

There was a shout, and the sound of running feet. But Ned must have been too fast for them, for a voice called out:

"Come back here, Lemuel. Let him go, we've enough to do with the she-bear."

"Aye," said another voice. "And if he comes back we'll set the dogs on him." There was laughter then, and the sound of dragging again. Dickon stood beside the cage, not moving.

The next moment the door was flung wide and he saw Osric framed in the opening.

Chapter Seven

A slow smile spread across Osric's face.

"Well, just look who's here," he said, his voice soft and crafty. "If it isn't our young master know-all come to see his bear cub. And brought your friend with you ... only he's run off, hasn't he?"

"The Master told me I was to come whenever I could," Dickon said. "I've done no harm."

"The Master told me..." Osric mocked him. "I've done no harm."

He came no closer, but stood, leaning against the door jamb, and for a moment there was silence. Dickon saw Lemuel straighten up from the cage and stand, listening.

"Think you can blow in here just as you please, do you?" Osric asked, turning the whip he held in his hands. "Think you know all about bears, I daresay, more than us who've been working here for years." His eyes narrowed.

Dickon swallowed and shook his head. He had to catch Ned. If he ran, perhaps he might not be too late.

"Your pardon, but I have to go now," he said, taking a step towards the door. Quick as lightning Osric shot out his arm to bar the way.

"Like bears, do you?" he asked.

Dickon watched him steadily.

"Please let me pass," he said.

For an answer Osric uncoiled the whip and cracking it once in the air sent it flying in an arc that looped and circled around Dickon. He gasped as the lash thudded against his ribs, and, winded for a moment, felt himself being hauled in like a landed fish.

"I asked you a question," Osric said softly, his face close. "Do you like bears? Take care how you answer now, for I have a particular reason for asking."

Dickon gritted his teeth, reaching for breath.

"Best let the boy go, Osric," Lemuel said, stepping up to the door. "We're needed back in the ring."

"Presently," Osric said. "I have a score to settle first."

Dickon felt fear take hold of him. "Let go of me," he gasped, beginning to struggle. "Let go!" But the whip bound him fast. Osric smiled.

"Think you can come in here all mealy mouthed and steal the Master's favours, don't you? Oh yes, I heard him offer you silver ... and for what? Teaching that bear's whelp to do tricks, bringing in sweet cakes and feeding it by hand. Pah!" His eyes were slits now, and he jerked on the whip, pulling Dickon closer still so that their faces were almost touching. "Well, you don't fool me with your trickery," he went on. "You're nothing but a scrubby little tanner's 'prentice, and seeing as you're here and there's none about but Lemuel and me, I've made up my mind to settle the matter once and for all. You like the cub well enough, let's see how you get along with its dam." He gave a low chuckle. "You'll need all your charms with her, I'm thinking. Fresh from the ring, she's not in a pretty mood."

Still holding Dickon fast, he reached for the bunch of keys at his belt, and began to drag him towards the cage.

"No!" Dickon gasped in sudden terror, seeing at last what Osric meant to do. "No! No!"

"But I say yes," Osric answered grimly. "You'll not come sniffing around here after today, I fancy."

"Osric, I like not this," Lemuel cut in. "Beat him if you will, but let him go."

"Keep your mouth shut, you fool. And fetch in the she-bear."

"'Tis you that's the fool," Lemuel retorted. "When the Master finds out..."

"The Master will find out nothing but what we tell him: that the boy climbed into the cage from the hay loft up there, and when he heard us coming hid himself in that pile of straw, not knowing that we would put the she-bear in with the cub."

"But I will tell him the truth," Dickon gasped.

"Will you now?" Osric smiled, twisting the key in the lock as he spoke. "I doubt it. I doubt you'll say much at all after you've faced the wrath of the wounded she-bear. 'Twill be a while before the Bear Ward comes to see to her. And by then..."

A scream was beginning in Dickon's throat. He started to open his mouth, but Osric was too quick for him. Clapping a hand over Dickon's face he swung open the door of the cage, and with hideous strength threw him inside.

The last thing Dickon remembered was the look on Osric's face, and the crack as his head hit the ground. Then everything went dark.

The little beast with two legs lies on the ground and does not move.

Now I can smell blood. There are shouts and there is roaring. The roaring is my mother, and the blood is her blood. The big beasts with two legs pull her into the cage and she howls in pain. Her fur is dark with the blood, her flesh has been torn. The big beasts with two legs chain her to the wall. She tries to strike them with her claws, but the fight has gone from her and they are too quick.

They have gone now, and left the little beast lying on the ground. Still he does not move.

My mother's roars fill the darkness. They tell of blood and fear and many hurts. I want to go to her, but when I get close she strikes at me. In her madness she does not know it is me. I run back to the straw pile and watch her.

Now she is snuffing the air. She can smell the little beast with two legs and she roars again. I know that she will attack him. But he cannot smell the danger as I can. He doesn't move. She sways her head and growls. Her growl is like a moan. I have heard that sound before. It is the sound of the hunting bear. In her rage she means to kill the little beast. I see the dark shape of her as she rises on to her hind legs.

But she must not attack the little beast. He means her no harm, and the big beasts have hurt him. That is why he lies so still.

I growl. My mother stops, turns her head, looks down at me. I growl again. Now I come closer to the little beast. Now I sit beside him. Still he does not move. My mother watches me. Softly, softly I lay my paws across his back, first one, then the other. I must make my claws gentle so as not to hurt him. His body is warm. I stare at my mother.

Now I feel my limbs grow strong. If my mother tries to claw him I will stop her. I growl again so that she will understand. My mother stares back at me.

Long time we stay like that. Then my mother sways her head, drops on to her front paws again and turns away. That means I have won.

Long time, long time the little beast does not move. He is not dead. I feel the breath in his body. Now he makes a moan. . .

Someone was groaning, someone close by. Dickon could hear the sound quite clearly. He wanted to open his eyes to see who it was, but his head was throbbing too much. And there was a weight on his back. Something held him down.

The groan came again when he tried to move.

That's me, he thought. I am making that noise on account of the pain in my head. It's surely bleeding.

Gingerly he lifted his hand. And felt … fur. And something wet against the back of his hand.

There were footsteps then, and voices coming closer, and a light behind his eyelids.

"Lord have mercy," said a deep voice. "What sight is this?"

"The boy is surely dead," said a second voice.

"Or fainted away from fright," said the first voice. "But how came he here? And the cub…"

As though in answer Dickon heard a growl, soft and low, which seemed to come from just above his head. And then, from a little further off, a rustle and a deep-throated roar.

That roar sent a thrill of fear through him, and brought him to his senses at last. He knew now where he was, and opening his eyes he saw, by the light of the lantern, the great she-bear rearing up on her hind legs in the far corner of the cage, and towering over him. He gave a moan of terror.

"He lives," said the first voice. "Quick, hand me that stave! And fetch the Master. Hurry!"

It was too late, Dickon thought. Already the bear was getting ready to strike. And he could not move.

But before she could reach out to him there came another low growl. The weight lifted from his back, and he saw the cub, his cub, land with a thud on all four paws between him and the she-bear. Swaying its head from side to side it stood growling up at her. For a moment the she-bear hesitated, and in that moment Dickon heard the man shout to him.

"Roll away! Now, boy! Quick ... over here by the bars ... she'll not reach you here. The chain is too short."

With one sick, dizzying lurch Dickon forced himself to move. He rolled, once, twice, and felt iron against his back as he reached the bars. Something was clanging near his head, and above the roaring of the she-bear there came the rattle of the cage door being opened. Then a hand stretched out and pulled him free. He felt himself being carried a little way off and then laid gently on the ground.

" 'Tis all right, lad," said the voice. "You're safe now."

Dickon could do no more than nod, for his head swam and when he opened his eyes the bars of the cage seemed to dance before his eyes. Somewhere beyond the circle of light there were dim, shadowy figures, and voices speaking low. Darkness was closing in on him.

"Water!" said the deep voice of his rescuer. "He is like to faint."

The ice cold shock of it brought him to his senses

again. He was aware of a thick, strong arm around him and the corner of a leather apron where the man knelt beside him on the ground. Then there was a movement by the door, and the Master shouldered his way past the group of men outside and strode into the pool of light.

"How now, Bear Ward, what's this to-do that I must be sent for after a hard day's work?" he began, and then, seeing Dickon on the ground, he came quickly forward and bent down towards him. "How came you here, Dickon?" he asked. "Are you hurt?"

"You know the lad?"

"Aye, well enough," the Master answered. "Can you stand, Dickon? Answer me, boy, can you stand?"

"I think so," Dickon answered, moving a little. But it was no good. His legs still felt like straw, and the dizziness came back.

"Steady there, lad," said the gruff voice. "You'll do well enough bye and bye." The Master straightened up with a frown.

"Is he badly hurt? I see no blood."

"Stunned, Master, but not wounded. See, he has a lump here, on his temple. We found him when we came to dress the she-bear's wounds. At first I thought he was dead. He was lying inside the cage, on the ground."

"Inside the cage? But. . ."

"Aye. How he came there I know not. The cage was locked."

"Locked, you say?"

"Aye, 'twas a miracle we came when we did." The Bear Ward cleared his throat with a rumble. "The strangest thing of all was that the cub seemed to be protecting him," he went on, his voice puzzled. "You will think me a block-head, Master, but I swear. . ." He stopped, and cleared his throat again.

"Aye . . . go on," the Master urged.

"I'd not have believed it unless I'd seen it with my own eyes," he continued. "The cub had its paws across the lad's back, just sitting there and staring at the she-bear, like it was telling her to let the lad alone."

It was quiet for a moment. The Master stood, stroking his chin.

"Go on," he said.

"Well, before I could get to the lad, the she-bear went up on her hind legs. I thought he was done for then, I can tell you, lying like a stone on the ground. But the cub was having none of it. It gave a growl, and –"

"Aye?"

"And jumped between her and the lad. Stopped her, just long enough for me to shout to the boy to roll away, for he had come to himself by then and saw what would happen if he didn't move." He paused, looking down at Dickon, his craggy face puzzled. Then he shook his head. "I tell you, Master, 'twas the strangest thing I ever did see."

A kind of wonder was beginning to steal over Dickon. Propped against the Bear Ward's arm his gaze crept across to the small dark shape that lay crouched inside the cage. He didn't know how long he had lain on the ground after Osric threw him in there, but one thing was certain. The cub had saved his life.

"Strange indeed," said the Master in a low voice. "It seems as though the Bear Catcher was right in what he said. The lad has some special power. What think you, Bear Ward?"

The Bear Ward shook his head.

"I know not, Master. But I never saw the like of it before."

The dizziness had almost gone now. Dickon sat up straighter. Outside it had grown dark. Curfew must have sounded long since, he thought. Ned would be back at the tannery and telling them everything. What was he to do? If he went back there, he would never see the cub again. But there was danger at the Bear Garden, too; danger for him and the cub. Osric had wanted him dead. Now that the cub had saved his life, things would be worse than ever.

Seeing him move, the Master bent to look at him.

"Well, can you stand now, boy?"

"I think so," Dickon nodded.

"Good," the Master nodded, when the Bear Ward had helped him up. "And now, tell me how you came to be in the cage. Not even your special powers can allow you to pass through a locked door, I think."

Dickon frowned.

"I have no special powers," he muttered. "The cub trusts me, that's all."

"Ah, so it was the cub that unlocked the door of the cage and let you in, was it?" Dickon opened his mouth and then closed it again. "Answer me, boy," the Master continued, taking Dickon's chin in his hand and looking down into his face. "There is some mystery here, and I mean to get to the bottom of it."

It would be best to lie, Dickon thought desperately. If he didn't give Osric away, perhaps the man would stop hating him. He looked at the hay loft, measuring the drop from the edge of the loft to the cage below. But it was too far. He would have been mad to try and jump from there. The Master would never believe him.

"Best tell the truth," the Bear Ward said quietly, laying a steadying hand on Dickon's shoulder. "No harm will come to you, lad."

Seeing him properly now for the first time, Dickon looked into the seamed and craggy face that stared kindly down at him and knew that the Bear Ward was someone he could trust. After a moment he nodded and took a deep breath.

"I came to see the cub," he began, turning back to the Master. "You told me I could, whenever I was free."

"Aye," the Master nodded. "Go on."

"I was here, talking to it," Dickon went on. Then he stopped.

"Go on, lad," said the Master. "What then?"

But Dickon was staring across the barn to where Osric had suddenly appeared round the door, his face as white as chalk.

"Your pardon, Master..." he began.

With a grunt of annoyance the Master swung round.

"Well?" he said impatiently. "What is it now?"

"A man to see you, Master, on pressing business, he says, that will not wait. A man, Master, and his wife. He says he comes from the tannery in Twill Lane. Says he's looking for his boy – that boy. . ." He jerked his head towards Dickon. "Vows you've stolen him away."

Outside, the hubbub of voices was coming closer.

"Master Nashe," Dickon gasped, and forgetting everything else in that moment, he put out his hand and seized the Master's sleeve. "My master and his mistress. If they find me, they will stop me from coming here ever again. I'll never see the cub any more ... and I'll never be able to teach it to dance. Please, please, don't let them find me."

The fear must have shown plain on his face, for the Master gave a quick nod.

"Leave all to me," he said, and then, spinning round he said to Osric, "Tell Master Nashe I will wait upon him at once. Now! Go! And keep them outside! And you," he went on, turning to Dickon, "up to the hay loft. Go with him, Bear Ward, and see that he is well hidden in the straw. He can stay there until the morning. Make haste." He strode quickly towards the door.

Without waiting for Dickon to climb the ladder, the Bear Ward picked him up and, slinging him over his shoulder as though he had been a feather pillow, he carried him up the ladder.

"Down here, where you won't be seen," he said quietly, making a hollow for Dickon in the straw and covering him over. "And bide quiet till I come back for you."

Dickon heard the thud of his feet and the creak of the ladder as he went down again. The next moment Master Nashe must have pushed his way into the barn with Mistress Nashe at his heels, for their voices were just below him.

"Where is he?" Master Nashe was shouting. "Where is the boy? I'll have the magistrates on you for this, sir, you see if I don't."

"Calm yourself, good Master Nashe, calm yourself and tell me what you mean. Boy? What boy?"

"MY boy," Master Nashe shouted. "My apprentice."

"Dickon, by name," Mistress Nashe cut in. "A good for nothing, lazy, wicked boy, if ever there was one. A red-headed boy who brings trouble wherever he goes."

"But I know of no such boy," the Master answered.

"Well, then you lie, sir," Master Nashe interrupted. "For he was here not two hours ago, and with your permission. My boy Ned has come running back to tell us of it, half out of his wits with fear."

"With fear?" the Master asked.

"Aye, with fear. For this apprentice, OUR apprentice, mark you, has bewitched your bear cub, that very cub in there, which feeds from his hand like a pet lamb. The boy Ned has seen it with his own eyes. And you, sir, have set him on to do this."

Dickon heard the Master give a chuckle.

"'Tis no laughing matter," Mistress Nashe bellowed. "'Tis the devil's work, I'd say. And unless you bring us the boy we mean to fetch the magistrate."

"By all means fetch the magistrate, Mistress. But it will do no good. As you can see, the boy is not here. Only the cub and its dam which my Bear Ward is tending. She fought well today, but the dogs have done their work, and she is not in the best of tempers. I advise you both to stand back."

There was a menacing growl from below, and Dickon heard Mistress Nashe give a muffled scream.

"Back, back," the Master commanded. There was a shuffle of footsteps. "Aye, you'll be safe enough there," he went on. "Now, a red-headed boy, you say?"

"Carrot-headed," Mistress Nashe answered, but more faintly now.

"Let me think ... there was a boy," the Master went on after a moment. "A red-headed boy, who brought a letter from you."

"That is the one," Master Nashe exclaimed. "You have seen him?"

Dickon's heart had begun to pound.

"Aye, on that day. But today ... we have had a baiting today; you will understand that I have not been at leisure to look for red-headed boys."

"He was here," Master Nashe said obstinately. "Ned told us so."

"I will ask amongst my men and send word if I hear anything of him," the Master cut in. "But mark my words, 'tis the Fair that has kept him from home. And as for your other lad, well..." he chuckled again. "No doubt the two of them cooked this story up between them as a jest. By now your red-headed boy will be back at the tannery, as full of gingerbread as a rootling pig is of acorns, and sleeping in his bed."

"If 'tis so – " Master Nashe began.

But Mistress Nashe cut in, "I tell you, husband, I like it not. He's hiding somewhere hereabouts, I dare swear it."

"If so, he will come out when he's hungry," the Master replied. "Then I will box his ears and send him home for you to beat. But have no fear, Mistress. 'Tis my belief you'll find him back at the tannery when you return. 'Tis the Southwark Fair has brought this about. Mark my words; it sends the 'prentices half out of their wits with foolery."

"True enough," growled Master Nashe.

"But by Monday morning all will be well again, eh? And now, good Master, before you leave, about that bear pelt I promised you..."

Their voices faded into the distance and Dickon heard the barn door close.

For the moment, at least, he was safe.

Chapter Eight

Dickon closed his eyes. It was warm in the straw, and comforted by the sound of the Bear Ward moving about below him, he drifted off to sleep.

The creak of the barn door woke him and he sat up with a start, his head throbbing. Footsteps came towards the ladder, and there was a shaft of light from a lantern.

"You can come out now, lad," said the deep voice. "All's well. . ."

"Have they gone?" Dickon asked, relief flooding over him as he saw the craggy face appear at the top of the ladder.

"Aye, an hour since, and none the wiser," the Bear Ward nodded. "You've been asleep, my lad."

"You don't think they guessed?" Dickon asked, wanting to be certain.

"Not they," the Bear Ward chuckled. "They went off mightily pleased at the bargain they had made with my master for bear pelts."

Dickon frowned. "But when they find out I'm not there. . ."

"Hush now," the Bear Ward grumbled softly. "See, I brought you some bread and meat. And something to soothe your head as well. How do you feel?"

"Better," Dickon said. "Much better."

"And hungry?" he asked, putting down a platter of bread and meat beside the lantern. Dickon's mouth watered at the sight of the food, for he had eaten nothing since the morning. He took a piece of bread and some of the beef, and as he ate the Bear Ward sat at the top of the ladder, watching him. After a while, seeing that his hunger was satisfied, he gave a nod.

"And now let's take a look at that bump," he said, and kneeling down beside Dickon he ran his hands over his head. They were big hands, as big as hams, but gentle too. All the same, Dickon winced.

"Aye," he said. "I feel it. 'Tis the size of a pigeon's egg. But I have a salve here will cure that." He reached into the pocket of his leather apron and brought out a small bottle, and drawing the cork from it with his teeth, he poured a few drops of the dark brown oil into the palm of his hand.

How well Dickon remembered the smell of that oil! One sniff of it and he was back in his father's stable, watching Jacob at work.

"I know that stuff," he said, the words tumbling out before he could stop them. "My father's servant, Jacob, he used it on the mare when she went lame."

The Bear Ward's hands were still for a moment, and he looked curiously down at Dickon.

"Jacob?" he asked. "You say your father's servant was called Jacob?"

Dickon nodded.

"He works at the theatre now, since my father died."

"Aye, the Globe," the Bear Ward said, finishing his work and screwing the cork back into the bottle.

"You know him?" Dickon asked in surprise.

"Aye, I know Jacob." A slow smile creased his face. "And as for you, you must be Richard Stronge's lad, I'm thinking."

"That was my father's name," Dickon nodded.

"A fine man, God rest his soul."

"You knew my father?" Dickon asked in amazement.

For answer, the Bear Ward reached out his huge hand, and taking Dickon's shook it heartily.

"Fulke's my name," he said. "Pleased to make your acquaintance, Master Richard."

"Dickon."

"Dickon, then," he nodded. "But a second Richard Stronge before long, eh, when you are come to manhood?" He let go of Dickon's hand at last, and sat back, looking at him. "Well, bless my soul," he said. "Why, your father and I sailed many voyages together; that's how I come to know Jacob, too. I was aboard the Merry thought then, you must understand, serving under Captain Jones. Those were good days," he went on, with a shake of his head. "But times change, eh lad? And now that I am a married man I have slung my hammock, so to speak, and found work here."

Dickon leaned forward.

"And my father spoke to you of me?" he asked.

"Aye, that he did, and of your sister."

"Ann," Dickon nodded.

"Never a voyage home but he had some gifts to show that he was bringing back for you," Fulke went on. "Let's see ... I remember a flute."

"This one," Dickon broke in. He had forgotten it until then, but now, reaching inside his shirt, he pulled it out and unwrapping it from the cloth showed it to Fulke.

"You have it still," Fulke said, reaching out his finger to touch the carved wood, and Dickon nodded. "Your father would be glad of that, I think," Fulke went on, looking up at Dickon. "He was always proud of you, and boasted many a time how clever you were at your books."

Dickon turned away.

"That is all over now," he said, feeling the old anger well up inside him. "My stepfather, he had me apprenticed to Master Nashe, the tanner. I hate it there."

"So now you are a runaway apprentice," Fulke said after a moment.

"I didn't mean to run away," Dickon said, wrapping the flute in its cloth again and putting it back inside his shirt.

"Maybe 'tis not too late to go back," Fulke said, giving him a considering look. "There would be a whipping in it, no doubt, but that's not much, and soon over."

"I wouldn't mind the whipping," Dickon frowned. "I wouldn't even care if they put me in the stocks ... that's what they do to runaway apprentices, isn't it?" Fulke nodded. "But if I go back I will never see the bear cub again."

"Happen not," Fulke agreed.

For a moment there was silence. Dickon frowned once more. In his mind's eye he seemed to see the tannery in Twill Lane grow smaller and further off until at last it dwindled away into the distance, and suddenly he knew that he no longer had any part in it. Whatever the future held, his life there was finished. He took a deep breath and looked up at Fulke.

"I will never go back," he said.

"'Tis a hard thing to be a fugitive," Fulke said, his voice troubled. "And all on account of the bear cub, seemingly."

"You saw what happened," Dickon said, leaning forward. "The cub saved my life. We belong together now."

"Master seems to think so," Fulke nodded. "He has plans for you, and for the cub."

"I shan't let it fight," Dickon said fiercely. "Not ever. I saw what they did to the she-bear today."

"Aye, 'tis a cruel sport," Fulke agreed. "But the wounds heal quicker than you'd think; the she-bear will live to fight another day. But 'tis strange how deep you feel for that beast," he went on thoughtfully, his craggy face puzzled. "And the cub for you, it seems; now *that* I can't explain."

"But you don't think I've bewitched it, do you?" Dickon said, leaning forward.

"Not I," Fulke replied. "But there's some who might ... some who are muttering already of black magic and the devil's work. Now I don't believe in all that trumpery, 'tis nothing but moonshine and fiddle faddle to my mind. What's more, I've a fair idea of how you came to be inside a locked cage, which no doubt you'll tell the Master himself when he talks to you in the morning." He paused for a moment, and then went on. "But what I'm saying, young master, is this, I don't want you to come to more harm. And this is no place for you."

Dickon frowned.

"I can't leave the cub now, no matter what happens."

Fulke didn't answer, but sat for a while wrapped in thought. Then, suddenly, he slapped his hand against his leather apron with a smack that made Dickon jump.

"There's one who might help us solve this puzzle," he said. "What do you say if I go and find Jacob? He'll be drinking a pot of ale at the Anchor about now, I'm thinking."

"Jacob knows something of this already," Dickon said eagerly. "He was to meet me here tomorrow."

"We'll not wait until tomorrow," Fulke said. "I'll go and fetch him back here now. Then we can talk the whole thing over between us. What say you to that, young master?"

Dickon nodded eagerly. Jacob would know what to do. He always did. And in the meantime Dickon sensed that he could trust Fulke as completely as the bear cub trusted him.

After Fulke had gone, leaving him the lamp for company and promising to be back within the hour, Dickon finished the rest of the bread and meat and settled down comfortably in the straw. "I will see the cub every day now," he thought contentedly, half drifting off to sleep again.

Some time later he heard a creak, and the growl of the bears below as the barn door scraped open. He sat up.

"Fulke..." he whispered. "Fulke ... is that you?"

But the face that appeared at the top of the ladder wasn't Fulke's. Nor was it Jacob's.

"Seems you weren't expecting me," Osric said. "Thought it would be old Fulke, did you?"

The words hung in the air, and for a long moment there was silence. Dickon took a deep breath.

"What do you want?"

Osric smiled.

"I never was one to leave a job half done," he said quietly. "So when I see Fulke leave a while back, and the Master out to supper, I guessed you would be all alone up here. 'Osric,' I says to myself then, 'Osric, my lad, you'd best go back there and finish what you started. Now will be the time, before any more harm is done.'"

"I don't know what you mean." Dickon's mind was racing. It couldn't be long now before Fulke came back with Jacob. If he could just keep Osric talking.

"You know all right," Osric nodded, hoisting himself further up the ladder. "Stands to reason, after what happened this afternoon." His eyes moved to the empty plate which lay beside the lantern. After a moment he looked back to Dickon. "Told Fulke all about it, did you? Like you were going to tell the Master, only I stopped you just in the nick of time."

"The Master doesn't know," Dickon said. "No one need ever know."

"No one ever will," Osric said, smiling unpleasantly.

Dickon sat still, straining his ears for the sound of footsteps. How long had he been asleep? It must be nearly an hour since Fulke had left. Osric watched him through narrowed eyes.

"No use expecting old Fulke to come back," he

said. "He's gone to the ale house. 'Tis his way after a baiting. He'll be drinking there until the landlord throws him out at daybreak. And by that time, it will be too late."

For a moment Dickon's heart misgave him. Suppose it was true. Suppose Fulke did not come back. He swallowed.

"So you see we're all alone," Osric went on. "And this time there will be no mistake, no Lemuel to go dragging Fulke at his heels to tend the she-bear before 'twas needful, no Fulke to open the cage door. Just you and me."

"You're wrong about Fulke," Dickon said, lifting his chin. "He is coming back, and soon. He told me – "

"Quiet, devil's brat," Osric cut in, his voice soft and low. "No more of your tricks. First you bewitched the she-bear's whelp. Now you have bewitched the Master."

Dickon shook his head. "That's not true," he said.

"Why else does he mean to keep you? Come hell or high water, so he says. Well now, that doesn't suit me," he went on, "because sooner or later you may take it into your head to tell him how you came to be in that cage ... and what will happen to poor Osric then?"

"I swear not to tell him," Dickon said. "I swear it. He'll never know."

"Do you think I believe that?" Osric spat, and hate gleamed in his eyes. Then, slowly, he drew a knife from his belt. "I should have slit the cub's throat while I had the chance," he said. "I've a mind to do it yet."

"No," Dickon cried. "No!"

"You'd not like that, would you?" Osric smiled, holding the knife towards the lantern and turning it slowly, so that the blade glinted in the light. "Well, no matter. I have a better plan now. A plan that will settle you and the bear cub in one ... aye, and the dam too. And the best of it is that no blame will ever come to me."

For a moment he half closed his eyes, and a dreamy look came over his face.

"Did you ever see a burning?" he asked.

Dickon shook his head.

"I saw a witch burned once," he said. "A maid, that one was. Her name was Jennet. They burned her cat, too. 'Twas a wondrous sight, the beast shrieked as the devil came out of it." Dickon shuddered, drawing further back into the straw. "She was young, like you," the voice went on. "First they ducked her, and then they burned her." He gave a dreamy smile.

Then his eyes narrowed and he leant towards Dickon. "Magic, isn't it? That power you have over the cub. A spell, maybe. Is that why you played your music for it? Tell Osric, I should like to know."

"But it's not true," Dickon tried. "You know it's not true. There is no magic. The bear cub trusts me, that's all."

"Trust!" His voice rose. "Trust between a boy and a savage beast! You lie... 'tis the devil's work you do. So, say your prayers, devil's brat, to whoever you wish." He laughed. "The world will be well rid of you. A pity no one will ever know it was Osric who did the good deed."

Suddenly Dickon knew what he meant to do, and understood why he had talked of the burning of witches. But it was too late to stop him, for with a lightning movement Osric reached out his hand towards the lantern, and seizing the rushlight from inside it, he leant forward and thrust it deep into the pile of straw.

"No!" Dickon gasped, scrabbling backwards. "No!"

But already there was a bright tongue of leaping flame between them.

"Burn, witch, burn," Osric crooned.

Dickon could no longer see him, but above the

splutter of the flames there came a laugh, high pitched and eerie. It faded into the distance and died away.

For a moment the terror of the flames held Dickon motionless. He heard the barn door close and the heavy thump of the bar being shot home, and then there came another sound ... a low, frightened squeal.

The cub ... he must rescue the cub.

He tore off his surcoat and began to beat at the flames, but the fire had already taken hold of the straw and a choking cloud of smoke wreathed and coiled about him, making him cough. Covering his head with his surcoat, he began to crawl round the blaze, one hand stretched out in front of him, feeling for the edge of the hay loft. If he went too fast, he might fall over. After what seemed a long time his hand reached space. But which way was the ladder, left or right? Dickon had lost his bearings. He ran his fingers along, first one way, then the other, groping for the rungs, while behind him the flames crackled and sputtered, and the smoke grew thicker. He could hardly breathe. If Osric had moved it... For a moment he wrenched the surcoat away from his face, and in that moment he saw the struts of the ladder, lit by the flames, no more than a hand span to his right.

Shaking now, and coughing with the smoke he half climbed, half tumbled down until he reached the ground. He ran to the cage. But it was locked. Inside, the she-bear was roaring in terror, chained tight, poor beast, and hardly able to move. But the cub's chain was long and it ran hither and thither, squealing and hurling itself against the bars.

He leapt towards the door, beating on it with his fists, pushing with all his might against it, over and over again. But outside the bar still held.

"Fire," he shouted. "Help... Fire! Fire!"

There was no answer. Only running round and round inside his head the words:

"Burn, witch, burn..."

He was like to burn, too. Above him the loft was all ablaze. He could see flames snaking along the beams, and the smoke made it hard for him to breathe. Someone must come... Someone... Where were Fulke and Jacob? Soon it would be too late.

"Fire!" he shouted again, his voice hoarse. "Fire! Ho!"

But still no one came. At last, worn out with shouting, he ran back to the cage and sank to the ground with a sob. It was as close as he could get to the bear cub, although in its terror it didn't even know that he was near, but went on running up and down, howling. The cub had saved his life, and now he could do nothing to help it. Nothing.

"Burn, witch, burn..." Dickon whispered, leaning his forehead against the bars.

And then he heard it. The answering shout of "Fire!" from outside the barn, and the sound of someone calling his name.

He started to crawl towards the door. An instant later it was flung open and as the smoke billowed around him, he was on his feet and staggering into the clean air.

"Master Dickon, Master Dickon... We thought you were done for."

He felt Jacob's arms go round him.

"The cub," he gasped, half choked by the smoke, pulling away and turning wildly to Fulke. "The key... Quick! I couldn't..."

But now the yard was full of running figures and Fulke didn't seem to hear him.

"Water!" he roared. "Fetch water." Dickon grabbed his arm.

"The cub..."

Fulke shook his head.

"I fear it may be too late, lad. Look behind you."

Turning his head, Dickon saw that the barn was red and roaring.

"No," he shouted, beginning to sob. "No...
No... we must get him out. Give me the key."

Fulke looked once more towards the barn. Then
with a nod he tore off his surcoat, and plunging it
into the water butt he ran, head down, back into the
smoke.

"I must go with him," Dickon gasped.

But Jacob held him back and would not let him go.

Around them men were running with buckets,
plunging them into the water butt and hurling them
towards the flames. But Dickon hardly noticed
them. He was only aware of Jacob's arm around him
as he stood, his gaze fastened upon the dark,
smoking cavern into which Fulke had disappeared.

"What happened?" Jacob asked. He shook his
head, unable to speak. The roof was ablaze now, the
rafters and all. Jacob looked up. " 'Tis going any
minute," he muttered. "The whole place will fall
down."

Dickon stood rigid, watching the doorway.

And then with a creaking groan the beams began
to sag. Jacob darted forward.

"Fulke," he cried at the top of his voice. "Come
out now!"

As though in answer there was a sound of
squealing, and through the smoke Dickon saw

Fulke's huge, shadowy figure stagger from the barn, the bear cub in his arms.

"Now all the saints be praised," Jacob muttered.

Dickon started forward, but Fulke seemed to see neither of them, as he stumbled on like a man in a dream, his face all blackened and the sweat pouring from him.

"After him," Jacob said. " 'Tis best we get further off."

As they reached the wicket gate they heard a shout from behind them and, turning round, they saw the main roof beam of the barn fall with a rending crash. A moment later a huge shower of fiery sparks rose high into the night sky, and from the heart of the fire came the screams of the she-bear. Dickon saw the cub squeal and struggle in Fulke's arms.

"Aye, 'tis too late for your poor dam now," Fulke muttered, wrapping his leather apron more closely around it. " 'Twas nearly too late for thee."

Dickon shuddered, and stretched out his hand to the cub, but nothing could calm it at that moment.

"We must get it from here or it will go mad with fear," he said.

"Or tear me to pieces," Fulke said. "Give me your belt, Jacob. I can't hold the poor young beast much longer."

Between them they managed to thread Jacob's belt through the cub's collar. Then, kneeling down, Fulke unwrapped his apron and let it go, handing the end of the belt to Jacob. The cub's eyes rolled and it bucked and cavorted, until at last it came to a shivering halt crouched in the shelter of the wicket. Fulke rose slowly to his feet and wiped the sweat from his face with the back of his arm.

"I am to blame for this," he said, before Dickon could thank him. "I should have hung the lantern on the nail. That way it would never have fallen over." He shook his head and turned wearily to look at the fire. "What will the Master say when he gets back and finds this?"

" 'Tis lucky there is little wind," said Jacob. "And what there is blows towards the bean field. The fire will not spread."

"God willing," Fulke nodded. Then he frowned.

He was staring back across the yard, and Dickon realised how strangely quiet it had grown. Only the dogs howled now, as the fire burnt lower, and the men, who had until then been running back and forth with buckets, were standing together in a group. In that moment Dickon knew that Osric was amongst them. He stood up.

"The lantern didn't fall over," he said urgently.

"It was knocked over ... by Osric. He set fire to the barn on purpose."

"With you inside it?" Jacob asked roughly. "Come, Master Dickon, that's not possible."

"It's true," Dickon said. "He was the one who threw me into the cage with the she-bear. He says I am a ... a witch!"

"A witch!" Jacob gave a short laugh.

"And he wants me dead," Dickon said.

Jacob looked at Fulke, who had stood listening. "Who is this Osric?" he asked.

"A man full of malice," Fulke answered. "A creeping, crafty, violent knave. The chief whipper of bears, who loves his work and despises all gentleness."

At that moment an angry murmur rose amongst the men.

"The Witch ... the Witch..."

"I don't like the sound of this," Jacob muttered.

"Nor I," Fulke nodded. "He works on the men, and with the Master away there is none to stop him."

"Of all things I hate a mob," Jacob grunted, his voice surly. "Unreasoning clods! Hark at them." Another murmur rippled through the crowd, and they stirred and shuffled.

"They will kill the cub," said Dickon. "We must do something."

"Aye," Jacob grunted. "Take to our heels, and sharpish, too."

Fulke nodded, swinging the gate open.

"I will try and hold them back," he said. "But it may not be for long. Leave the bear cub with me and run." But Dickon shook his head.

"I'm not going without the cub," he said. "If Osric catches it he will cut its throat."

"The cub ... the cub," Jacob grumbled. "As though you weren't in enough trouble."

"I would rather stay and face them myself," Dickon said obstinately.

"You'll not have long to wait, I'm thinking," Fulke said, jerking his head towards the men, who were already turning in their direction. "Go! Take the cub if you must, but go!"

And so, with Jacob holding the leather belt, and Dickon urging the cub from behind, they half pulled, half dragged it through the gate and out into the sheltering darkness beyond.

Fulke swung the gate closed behind them, and the last Dickon saw of him was his broad back as he turned to face the crowd of men.

Chapter Nine

In front of them, to their left, loomed the Bear Pit; behind them the shouts of the men, and only Fulke to stand between them. But the cub, understanding nothing, dragged and pulled with every step they took.

"This won't do," Jacob said, casting a quick look over his shoulder. "Fulke cannot hold them much longer; once through that gate and they'll be on us."

Already one of the men was trying to climb the fence.

"I know a place to hide," Dickon said, suddenly remembering. "Quick! We must make for the Bear Pit."

Between them they lifted the cub and stumbled towards the shadow of the building.

"There's a way in," Dickon whispered. "They'll not think of looking here."

"I hope you're right," Jacob grunted, "for there's no time to be lost."

Leaving the cub to Jacob, Dickon dropped on to his hands and knees and began to crawl along beside the wall, feeling for the loose board. Behind them the voices grew louder.

"Here it is," he gasped, pushing the board to one side.

Jacob knelt beside him.

"Aye, 'twill do for you and the cub," he nodded. "And 'tis the best we can manage for the present. In you go."

"What about you?" Dickon asked.

"Think I can fold up like a lady's kerchief, do you?" He pushed the leather belt into Dickon's hands. "Here, take this, and don't let go. I'll not be far off, never fear, and once this hue and cry dies down I'll be back for you."

Dragging the cub after him, Dickon crawled through the opening. Behind him, Jacob slid the boards back into position, and then he was alone with the cub in the pitch blackness.

It was cold now, but he felt the sweat begin to trickle down his back as he crouched there, holding tight to the leather belt. The cub tugged at first, and then grew still, quietly snuffing the darkness.

Outside Dickon heard the sound of running footsteps. Then voices.

"The Witch ... the Witch ... burn the Witch..."

His teeth began to chatter so loudly he thought they could surely be heard. He clenched his jaw. The voices were close now. One of them was Osric's.

"He's hereabouts, I warrant. He and the bear's whelp ... they can't have got far."

"They'll have made for the river," another voice said.

"More likely hiding under the hedgerow," said another.

"Aye, search the field," Osric said. "And the old fellow who was with them ... look out for him, too."

Jacob, Dickon thought. Oh, Jacob!

The voices faded into the distance, and for a time after that there was silence. He heard an owl screech, and then, far off, the cries of the men as they called to one another in the field, further away, and further. The cub moved in the darkness, and Dickon felt it begin to lick his hand.

The clock was striking ten before Jacob returned. Dickon counted the strokes, and as they died away he heard the sound of a low whistle. Beside him the cub shifted, lifting its head in the darkness. Dickon held his breath, listening. There was a scuffling noise outside. Then Jacob's voice said, low and grumpy: "Plague on it ... 'tis me, Master Dickon. Where are you?"

Dickon grinned with relief, and giving an answering whistle he pushed the board aside and put his head out.

By the light of the moon he could see Jacob standing a little way off.

"Over here," Dickon called in a low voice. Jacob swung round and hurried towards him.

"Out of there now, and that pesky cub. Make haste."

Dragging the cub after him Dickon crawled out on to the grass. His head had started to throb again, and he was so cold and stiff he could hardly stand. Jacob clicked his tongue, the way he used to do when he was grooming the mare, and kneeling down beside Dickon, began to rub the life back into his legs.

"Are you sure they've gone?" Dickon asked, his teeth beginning to chatter.

"Aye, for the present," Jacob nodded. "But they'll be back at first light." He looked up at Dickon. "That's not all," he went on soberly. "There's talk of magistrates ... and worse. Come morning you'll be hunted all over London and you'll not get far dragging that beast behind you."

"What is to become of me?" Dickon said, his voice hollow, while inside his head the words began again – *Burn, witch, burn. . .* "Osric will never give up."

"Likely not," Jacob grunted, "which is why I've been devising of a plot to get you clean away from here and out of harm's way, you and that pesky cub."

"But how?" Dickon asked. "Where can we go?"

"I've a plan that will serve well enough," Jacob told him. "Mind, it's cost me a week's drinking money at the Anchor, but I suppose I must expect to do without my own pleasures if I'm to serve you as I served your father before you. 'Twas the same when he was alive. No thought for poor Jacob. Nothing but trouble and work. There, can you walk now?"

"I think so," Dickon nodded.

"Good, for we should be away from here by now."

"Where are we going?"

"You'll see soon enough. First we must get the beast into this basket."

He dragged a clothes hamper from the shadow of the bushes nearby and, putting up the lid, took out a bundle which he tossed towards Dickon.

"Cloak," he said. "Warm . . . and a cap to cover up that red hair of yours. Now give us a hand with the

140

cub, young master. And make haste. They'll not wait for ever."

Dickon wanted to ask who would not wait, but Jacob would answer no more questions. Between them they lifted the cub into the basket, and as soon as the lid was closed and Dickon had put on the cloak and cap, they set off, each holding one of the rope handles at either side.

The moon was riding high in the sky and all was quiet as they retraced the path that Dickon had taken the first day he visited the Bear Garden, heading towards the river. When they reached the alleyway, Jacob stopped for a moment, and peered ahead at the dark cleft between the buildings. Then he gave a quick nod and they set off again down the alley. Somewhere a dog barked, and the bear cub stirred and shook inside the hamper so that it was hard to hold it steady. Dickon heard Jacob give a grunt. Then they were through the alley and standing beside the Anchor tavern with the broad ribbon of the river in front of them.

Jacob signalled to him to put the hamper down, and wiping his arm across his forehead, peered along the shadowy waterfront.

" 'Tis there," he nodded, and cupping his hand to his mouth gave a low whistle.

A little way off Dickon could see the outline of a wagon, and the next moment there came an answering whistle and a tall figure stepped from the shadows.

But before they could cross the cobbles, the door of the tavern was flung open. The sound of shouting and laughter came from inside, and two men appeared in the lighted doorway.

"Actors from the Globe," Jacob hissed. "Say nothing."

"You leave us too early, Will," a voice called from inside. " 'Tis not near midnight yet."

"But I must be up early tomorrow," the man answered with a laugh, and then, turning to go, he caught sight of them.

"Jacob," he said pleasantly. "What news? Have they found the apprentice yet?"

"Not as I hear," Jacob said. "He'll be hiding somewhere, no doubt."

"The apprentice who set fire to the barn?" the other man cut in. "They say he bewitches the bears."

"As to that I know nothing," Jacob grunted.

"As like as not it was some other who fired the barn," the first man said. "Apprentices are blamed for all ills when the Southwark Fair is on. For my part I hope the lad will get clean away, for I would not like to be in his shoes if he is caught." Dickon looked up, and for a moment their eyes met. Then the man smiled. "I have had to leave town in my time, too."

"This is the tumbler's lad," Jacob said, seeing him still looking at Dickon. "He speaks no English." He jerked his head towards the wagon. "They leave shortly and I have some clean clothes for them."

At that moment the bear cub moved inside the basket, and Dickon saw the other man frown. But before he could speak the first one clapped him on the shoulder

"Come, Tom, we must be off and leave these good people to go about their business. Good night, Jacob. See you in the morning."

"Aye, as like as not," Jacob muttered. "Good night."

"Good night, and good fortune go with you ... and the boy," he said, and then, linking his arm through his friend's they set off together along the riverside.

"A narrow squeak," Jacob said.

"He looked straight at me," Dickon said. "I think he knew."

"Maybe," Jacob frowned. "And maybe not. But

he'll say nothing. Not Will . . ." He broke off, looking towards the wagon. Dickon saw that the man had emerged from the shadows again and was beckoning to Jacob. "They're ready to leave," he said, picking up one end of the hamper. "Look sharp now, Master Dickon. The sooner you are in that wagon and away from here the better."

A moment later they had crossed the cobbled yard.

"This is my young master," Jacob said softly to the tall man who had come forward to meet them. "And that – in there. . ." he jerked his thumb towards the hamper, "is the bear cub."

"Magical bear cub," the man said in a soft, foreign accent. Then, giving Dickon a little bow, he said, "Sebastien . . . my name . . . Sebastien. You come with us now." He grinned. "To bear country maybe."

"No," Jacob said sharply. "To Deptford as we arranged."

A sudden weariness overwhelmed Dickon, and he leant against the wagon. Who were these people, and where was Jacob sending him? Deptford . . . it made him think of ships, though he couldn't remember why.

"What shall I do at Deptford?" he mumbled.

"You'll wait for me," Jacob said. He had pulled

144

out his purse and was counting coins into Sebastien's hand. "The wagon will go slowly enough," he went on after a moment. "With a fast horse I'll be there to meet you in the morning."

"And then?" Dickon frowned.

"Why, then you'll be out of the way of all magistrates, mobs and masters," Jacob said, with a nod of satisfaction.

By then a second man had joined them, and was listening.

"Come," Sebastien said. "The horse is ready. It is time to go. Bruno," he added, jerking his head towards the second man. "My brother, and Marie, my brother's wife, and little Rosa."

Dickon turned to look at the two faces which had appeared from inside the wagon, and saw, by the light of the moon, the girl he had met outside the Bear Pit that afternoon.

"You," he said. Rosa nodded and smiled at him.

"You know Rosa?" Sebastien asked.

"Tumblers," Dickon said, with a nod. "You're tumblers, aren't you?" He turned to look at Jacob.

But at that moment, from somewhere in the distance there came the sound of men's voices calling. Jacob jerked his head towards the noise, and Sebastien gave a quick nod.

"We go now," he said, and the next moment Dickon felt himself being hoisted into the wagon and stowed at the furthest end. The hamper was lifted in after him, and before he had even had time to say goodbye to Jacob, Marie had thrown some sort of cloth over him, the horse had been whipped up and the wagon began to creak and rumble across the cobbles.

At first fear held him tense. But there were no more shouts. Minute followed minute and still the horse plodded on, its hoof beats ringing steadily through the darkness. After what seemed a long time Dickon lifted the cloth and peered out. He could see Rosa and Marie sitting on the tailboard of the wagon, their backs towards him, and beyond them through the opening, the black tent of the sky, pricked with stars. Near him the cub creaked and whined inside the hamper. He shifted, moving forward a little so that he could put his fingers through the hole. There was an answering movement then, and he felt the cub's nose pressed trustingly against his fingers. Perhaps it sensed that they were leaving the Bear Garden never to return, for after a while it settled down inside the hamper and went to sleep.

Dickon wrapped the cloak close about him, and covering himself with the cloth once more lay listening to the sound of hooves clop–clopping onwards through the night until sleep took him, too.

When he woke it was broad daylight. The wagon had stopped and he was alone. Rosa and Marie had gone, and so had the hamper and the bear cub.

He started up, thinking at first that he had been tricked again. And then from somewhere outside the wagon he heard Rosa laughing. It was a happy laugh, full of sunlight and the joy of the morning, and suddenly Dickon felt happy too. He crawled to the back of the wagon and stuck his head out between the flaps of canvas.

It was a fine morning, pale and bright. Already the sun was scattering the early morning mist, and down below he could see the river, broader now and silver blue, with the tall masted sailing ships riding at anchor. Beside the wagon, which was drawn up on the grass, the road wound down towards Deptford. Sitting a little way off on the trunk of a fallen tree beside the stream were Sebastien, Bruno and Rosa, and next to them was the hamper, still closed.

"You sleep long time," Sebastien called out as Dickon jumped down from the wagon. "See, the sun is up."

"It is good you wake now," Rosa said, running across the grass and taking him by the hand. "Bear cub wants to come out ... goes grr ... grr..."

Dickon smiled at the way she screwed up her face, and then feeling suddenly shy, knelt down beside the hamper and began to undo the buckles.

"Is fierce, no?" Rosa asked, taking a step or two back as Dickon slid his hand carefully inside, searching for the cub's collar. "Bear cub bites, I think."

Dickon shook his head. Holding tight to the cub's collar, he slowly opened the lid of the hamper. Sebastien and Bruno watched him from the tree trunk.

To begin with the cub crouched low in the hamper and didn't move, but as Dickon talked quietly to it, stroking its ears, it lifted its head and stared solemnly round at the wonder of the new world that lay outside the hamper. Its nose twitched, and it began to snuff the air.

"Come," Dickon urged it softly. "Come, you can get out now. See ... it's quite safe."

He tipped the basket forward.

Slowly, first one paw and then the other was lowered on to the grass. Then it heaved its back paws out as well and stood, shuddering a little and blinking. For a moment no one moved. Rosa had stepped back. Now she stood still, staring at the cub, her dark eyes very round, and Dickon saw Sebastien lean forward, watching intently.

Taking hold of Jacob's leather belt which was still threaded through the cub's collar, Dickon started to lead it across the grass. It moved slowly at first, hesitating, sniffing at the dew on the daisies, and raising its snout to the freshness of the morning air. The horse paused for a moment in its grazing as they came near, lifting its head to stare, and then, seeing no cause for alarm, went on chomping.

And then, as though suddenly scenting something interesting, the cub turned and set off at a scamper towards the stream, tugging Dickon along behind.

"You're thirsty," he muttered. "Of course . . . but you can't drink with that thing on, can you?" He frowned, remembering how he had undone it the day before. Yesterday, he thought. That was yesterday. Someone, Fulke perhaps, had put it back on.

The instant the strap was off the cub crouched by the stream and began to drink, taking in draught after draught of water, and Dickon knelt beside it, cupping his hand over and over again to carry the cold, clear liquid up to his mouth until the tight, dry ache of the smoke had gone from his throat. Then he splashed the sunlit water over his head, not caring that the drops ran down the back of his neck, for there was no

Mistress Nashe to pummel at him that morning and call him Carrot Head. Instead he was here, with his cub, in a quiet green field; so quiet that he could hear the whisper of the golden brown leaves as they fell from the trees above and floated down the stream.

"We are free," thought Dickon. "The cub and I are free!"

Somewhere not far off a blackbird began to sing. And then the cub stopped drinking and, lifting its head, gave a low growl.

Dickon swung round. But it was only Rosa who had come tiptoeing softly across the grass, and was standing close by, watching.

"The cub means you no harm," Dickon said, seeing her take a step back.

She nodded, and then held out a coil of rope to him.

"Papa say you want this maybe?"

Dickon nodded gratefully, for his arm was aching from holding on to the belt, which was short enough. He threaded the rope through the cub's collar and tied it with a good knot, bidding it stay still till he had finished. When it was done the cub turned to look at him.

"Go on, then," he coaxed it, letting the rope go slack.

As though understanding, the cub gave a glad toss of its head, and waded out into the middle of the stream until the water reached its belly.

"It likes that," Dickon said, looking over his shoulder at Rosa.

"Now it will catch fish," she said, nodding solemnly.

Dickon smiled, and then frowned, wondering what bears did eat. He would have to find out. It had eaten Ann's cakes, and the apple. But what else? He was so busy thinking about it that he forgot to watch.

"See!" Rosa said, pointing, and turning his head Dickon was just in time to see a flash of silver as the cub scooped its paw out of the stream and threw the fish into the air, catching it between its jaws.

"You're right," he said wonderingly. "How did you know?"

"Papa told me," Rosa said, sitting down on the grass near him. "In my country are many bears. Papa has watched in the high mountains, and seen them catch the fish."

"Where is your country?" Dickon asked curiously.

"In France," she answered. "We go there now . . . on that ship." She pointed towards the harbour.

"You're going today?" Dickon asked.

"Soon," Rosa said, solemnly looking at Dickon. Then Sebastien called to her, and looking round Dickon saw Marie coming across the field with a pitcher and a loaf of bread.

"We eat now," Rosa said, jumping up. "I bring you food."

So it will end soon, Dickon thought, staring at the brightness of the sun on the water, and the cub splashing in the midst of it. They would sail away to France, Rosa and Sebastien and the others, and he would be left behind, a runaway apprentice and his bear cub. He glanced back along the road, wondering when Jacob would come. But the road was empty, and there was no sound of hooves.

He sat watching the cub until Rosa came back with milk in a bowl, and fresh, crusty bread. Dickon was glad of the food, for he had eaten nothing since the bread and meat that Fulke brought him the evening before. It seemed like a bad dream now, the barn and the fire, and Osric.

"What you do now?" Rosa asked after a while, brushing the crumbs from her skirt and giving him a sidelong look. "Where you go?"

Dickon shook his head.

"I don't know," he said. "I can't go back to London, that's certain, not now I'm a runaway." He frowned, staring down at the rope between his hands.

Rosa leant forward.

"You come with us maybe," she said, her eyes sparkling. "You like that ... no? To be a tumbler, like us?"

Dickon stared at her. Then he looked away.

"If only I could," he said. "But what would happen to the cub? We have to stay together, you see."

Rosa nodded quickly.

"Bear cub come too," she said eagerly. "You like?"

It was impossible. But Dickon found himself smiling and nodding just the same.

"Yes," he said. "Yes."

"Good. I ask Papa and Bruno now," Rosa said, as though it was the easiest thing in the world. And jumping up she ran over to where they were sitting and began talking to them, giving little skips of excitement and waving towards Dickon.

Dickon couldn't bear to look. To be a tumbler, to go with them, away from all this, to sail on that ship down there, he and the cub. But it was only Rosa's idea. They would never agree to it. He looked quickly over his shoulder. Rosa had her hands stretched out now, pleading. Dickon looked away again and stared at the cub.

It must have eaten enough fish by then, for it was clambering up the bank and as Dickon shortened the rope between his hands it began to shake the water from its coat, showering him with a cloud of silver drops.

He picked up the last of the bread and jumping up held it out to the cub. Perhaps it would remember.

"Sit," he said. "Sit!"

The cub twitched its snout.

"Sit," he said again. This time it gave a little grunt, stretching out towards the bread. "Sit!" Dickon said firmly. "Sit first, then bread." Slowly, as though remembering, it sank on to its haunches, looking up at him. "Good," Dickon nodded, giving it the bread.

Behind him the voices had stopped. When he turned round Rosa was beckoning to him excitedly.

Dickon took a deep breath and gathering up the rope he walked towards them.

"You teach cub to sit?" Sebastien asked. Dickon nodded.

"I can teach it to do other things, too," he said. "To beg, maybe. And to dance. It likes my music."

"You play music?" Sebastien asked, glancing quickly round at Bruno. "What kind of music?"

"Flute music," Dickon said.

"Show me!"

Through everything that had happened, it was still there, tucked deep inside his shirt, as though it was part of him. Dickon took the cloth off carefully and held the flute out for them to see.

"You play now," Sebastien said.

Dickon took the cub over to a nearby tree, and tied the rope to one of the branches. Then he came back and lifted the flute to his lips.

He played them a song of Wales, one of the songs his mother had taught him. It was a lilting melody, sad and sweet.

"You know more?" Sebastien asked when he had finished. "Music for dancing?"

His face was serious now, and he leant forward intently, with Rosa held in the crook of his arm. Bruno and Marie were still, too.

"I could play you a jig," Dickon said.

He could see Rosa's foot starting to tap as he played. After a while she pulled away from Sebastien, and began to dance, smiling and clapping her hands in time to the music and calling to Marie and Bruno to join her. Sebastien was smiling, too.

As Dickon reached the last notes he heard the sound of a horse's hooves coming fast along the road. He lowered the flute without turning round, and looked across at Sebastien.

Chapter Ten

*W*e are crossing the great water. When the wind blows, the cage that carries us along creaks and groans, and the white roof of it fills with the wind's breath and drives us onward, the little beast and me. In the dark time, the little beast unties the chain that binds me and we walk upon the floor of the cage and see the roof moving above us like clouds. The great water is close to us; when the cage rocks from side to side it splashes up on to the boards and wets our feet. In the dark time I see the stars shining in the darkness, beyond the white roof. They tell me we are going south ... south to the land of my birth ... south ... the wind brings the scents of the forest and the warm smell of the sun on the mountains. I feel it and am glad.

Sometimes the little she-beast walks with us, the one who calls me Nounou. It is not the name my mother gave me, but no one knows that name and my mother is gone from me for ever. Now my little beast calls me

Nounou as well. He is pleased when I look up, for he rubs my ears. The little she-beast is pleased, too, and claps her hands together. I understand, then, that it is my new name.

My little beast makes other sounds as well. Sit means I must go down on my haunches. Up ... and I must rise to my full height. Down ... and I drop on to all four paws again. I do all these things to please the little beast, for he is gentle in his ways. He brings me food and will let no one whip me. He has brought me out of the place of darkness and blood. And so I do his will.

But he is not as strong as I am, and nor is he wise in the ways my mother taught me. He does not snuff the air as I do. When a shoal of fish swims beside the wooden cage beneath the water he does not know it, and when the sea birds cry that a great rain is coming he cannot hear what they are telling. He cannot smell the warm south coming on the wind as I can. None of these things does he know, for though he is wise in the ways of men he cannot speak my language.

But still I do his will, for he has brought me out of that place of darkness and blood, of fire and pain, and wherever he goes, I will go.

Leaning against the side of the ship Dickon watched the narrow grey-brown rib of land approaching, and was heartily glad to see it, for his stomach had not been his own for the past two days.

At first, while the ship made its way through the English Channel, the water had been calm and flat, and as the sailors hoisted more sail to catch what little breeze there was, and grumbled that they were making little headway, he had thought what a fine thing it was to be on a sailing ship, just like his father before him. But two days out, as they rounded the north coast of France and came into the Bay of Biscay, the sky turned grey and the wind changed. Now Dickon felt the rain against his face. The water grew billowy, slapping against the sides of the ship so that it rocked and bucketed, while up above the sails tore and slapped and cracked in the north-westerly wind. Before long he had begun to feel mightily seasick, and being on a sailing ship no longer seemed such a fine thing after all. Wrapped in his cloak he lay huddled below decks beside the bear cub, wishing that he had never left England to take up the life of a tumbler.

"Biscay," Sebastien muttered, his face the colour of curds and whey. "Every time the same!" And as the ship pitched and shuddered again a fresh groan escaped him.

Bruno and Marie were propped against one of the

bales of woollen cloth a little way off, their eyes closed. Only Rosa seemed not to mind the rough sea, but spent most of the time on deck, coming down below occasionally to peer at them all and shake her head.

Sometime in the afternoon of the fourth day, the sea grew calm again, and the feeling of sickness left him. When Rosa came swarming down the rope ladder to tell him that land had been sighted and they would reach Mimizon before dark, Dickon splashed cold water on his face and, wrapping his cloak round him, followed her up on deck.

He could see the coastline clearly now. The rib of land had turned from grey-brown to green, and there was a church tower, and some houses, white against the evening sky.

"Mimizon," Rosa said, pointing. "France ... my home! Nounou's home, too, I think?"

"Perhaps you're right," Dickon said, turning to look at her. "The Bear Catcher came from France."

"You see!" Rosa clapped her hands. "He is a French bear, *le bon Nounou*, and soon he will be back in his mountains. Then he will be happy."

Dickon, who could see that she was happy to be coming home, nodded and smiled at Rosa. But her words troubled him all the same, for even when they reached the mountains the cub would not be free. It would still have to wear its collar and chain. It would have to learn tricks, to dance and beg for food. That was the bargain they had made, he and Jacob and Sebastien, standing together in the field above Deptford.

"A year," Jacob had said. "One year. You bring my young master back with you next Southwark Fair, or you'll have me to answer to."

"It's good," Sebastien had nodded. "My Rosa, she likes him."

"That's as may be," Jacob growled. "He'll put money in your pocket, too, I reckon, or you'd not be agreeing to take him."

"Perhaps," Sebastien smiled. "But not yet. Winter comes now. In winter stay at home and work ... make new acts." He turned to Dickon. "You teach bear cub to dance, yes?"

"Yes," Dickon had nodded.

"If you can," Jacob muttered.

"I will teach it," Dickon said, looking at Sebastien. "You'll see."

"Good," he nodded. "And in spring we travel ... work at fairs ... you play music and bear dances, yes?"

"And in September you come back to Southwark again," Jacob cut in, giving Sebastien a steady look.

"It's good," Sebastien nodded.

"Better than dangling on the end of a rope, I daresay," Jacob grunted.

Dickon looked across at the cub which was digging for something under the roots of the tree. They would be together always now, he thought, far from the Bear Garden. They would never go back there again. A new life stretched before them both, glittering and bright with promise. Or so it had seemed that morning.

And so it had been agreed, and the three of them had shaken hands on it.

Later, while the others packed up the wagon, Jacob drew Dickon aside.

"I warned you that beast would bring you nought but trouble," he said, giving Dickon a worried look. "Your sweet sister said the same. And now see what you've come to." He shook his head. "What would my master say, and you with your book learning and all."

"'Tis for the best," Dickon said. "I could never go back to the Bear Garden now, even if I wanted to. You said so yourself."

"Aye, that's true," Jacob nodded. "The hunt is

still on." He ran his hand over his head. "But, my young master . . . to be a fugitive."

"It's not so long," Dickon said. "A year, that's all. And this way the cub will be safe, and I can be with it."

"The cub . . . the cub," Jacob grumbled. "You think of nothing but that pesky beast. What of you?" Dickon, who could hardly believe his good fortune, said nothing. "Sebastien is a good man, mind," Jacob went on after a moment, "and the maid, well she's taken a liking to you, anyone can see that. But my master's son. . ." He shook his head. "To be a tumbler . . . what manner of life is that?"

"Better than skinning dead animals in Master Nashe's tannery," Dickon retorted.

"Well, happen you'll make something of it," Jacob said at last. "Myself, I never could abide that Butcher Tyndal."

They smiled at each other.

"Did you see Ann?" Dickon asked, as they walked over to Jacob's horse.

"Time enough for that once the ship has sailed," Jacob said.

"She will be worried," Dickon frowned. "They would have gone there. . . Master Nashe, and the magistrates . . . everybody."

"Now don't you fret about your sweet sister," Jacob told him. "When she hears all that I have to tell her, she'll be heart glad you have gone. Besides, you'll be back in a year. 'Tis not so long, and France is not so far."

"Oh, Jacob, I shall miss you," Dickon said in a sudden rush. "I wish you were coming with me. You could help me to train the cub."

"Just like your father," Jacob said, suddenly busy with the horse's reins. "Expect me to leave my own work at the theatre and follow you – "

"Would you?" Dickon asked eagerly.

But Jacob shook his head with sudden firmness.

"See here, young master, I've done what I can. From now on it's up to you. And if things don't go as you might wish, well, just you remember, I'll be waiting for you right here at Deptford in a year's time."

Dickon stared for a moment at the gnarled, brown old hands holding the reins of the horse, and thought of all the times he had watched those hands grooming his father's mare in the stable at home. Suddenly there was a lump in his throat. He swallowed and looked up.

"Perhaps I'll make my fortune," he said, through a blur of tears.

"Aye, perhaps you will," Jacob said gruffly, swinging himself into the saddle. "In the meantime, best see to that pesky cub of yours. It looks as if Sebastien is ready to leave."

Now, standing there on the deck with Rosa beside him and watching the harbour at Mimizon draw closer each moment, Dickon felt a sudden loneliness sweep over him. England, and everything he had known, seemed far away, and an ocean divided him from Jacob and Ann.

Rosa, sensing his sadness, put her hand on his arm.

"You are glad to see France, no?" she asked.

"I was thinking," Dickon said. "I can't even speak your language."

"I teach you," Rosa said quickly. "You teach Nounou, I teach you. *C'est très facile*."

"Faseel..." Dickon frowned.

"That mean ... it is very easy," Rosa laughed. "*C'est très facile*."

"*C'est très facile*," Dickon repeated.

"Good," Rosa nodded. "*Très bon*. Soon you speak French like me. Now we go and tell Nounou we are back in France." And pulling Dickon after her she ran towards the hatchway.

By the time they left the harbour darkness was

falling, and as soon as they were outside the town, Sebastien and Bruno began to look for a place where they could stop the wagon. Before long they came to a clearing at the edge of a forest of shaggy-topped trees, beside a small lake, and, turning off the road, Sebastien drew the wagon up near the water's edge.

Dickon had never spent a night in the open air before, and he soon discovered that there was much to do, and that each person had their own job. First the animals must be seen to and, while Bruno unhitched the horse from the wagon and led it down to the lake to drink, Sebastien helped Dickon to lift the hamper from the wagon. Letting the bear cub out, Dickon followed, a little distance from Bruno, so as not to alarm the horse, and holding fast to the rope that was threaded through the cub's collar, he let it drink its fill. He could see Rosa and Marie moving about under the trees, gathering wood to make a fire while Sebastien prepared the tinder box.

Soon the smoke began to rise, and as the cub splashed around, fishing for its supper in the lake, the smell of roasted meat mingled with the scents of the fire and the forest.

Marie had bought food before they left the harbour. There was bread, and soft cheese as well as the meat, and Dickon found that now he was back on dry land, he was hungrier than he had been since he left England. As they ate, the others talked softly in French, and he listened, not understanding, but content to watch the first bright stars appear in the sky and see the shifting red and gold of the camp fire as Rosa fed it with more sticks. He turned often to look at the cub, too, which was tied to the wheel of the wagon, and had settled down to clean its pelt with long, rasping strokes of its tongue, leaving off from time to time to stare up at the sky and snuff the night air.

After a while Rosa began to yawn, leaning against Sebastien's shoulder, and soon she was fast asleep. Shortly afterwards Bruno and Marie crept away and climbed up into the wagon. Dickon wondered where his bed was to be that night.

"Sleep now, beside fire," Sebastien whispered. "Warm here." And wrapping himself in his cloak and signalling to Dickon to do the same, he curled up on the ground with Rosa beside him.

Dickon lay for a long time, staring up at the stars and listening to the sounds of the forest as the darkness deepened and the fire burned low. At last, slipping away from the others, he crept over to the wagon and lay down beside the cub, feeling the warmth of its pelt against him, and fell at last into a dreamless sleep.

The next morning, as soon as the sun was up and the animals had been watered, they set off again along the road that led through the forest. Dickon sat up on the front of the wagon that morning, with Bruno and Sebastien, while Rosa and Marie rode on the tail. The sky was blue and a soft, warm wind ruffled the tops of the trees. Dickon could hear Rosa's voice and sometimes her laugh rang out above the sound of the horse's hoofs on the road, but neither Bruno nor Sebastien spoke much until they had left the forest behind them.

"Picking grapes," Sebastien said, seeing Dickon straighten up and gaze about him at the flat, wide countryside of open fields that they were passing, and he pointed with his whip towards a group of people working nearby. They looked up as the wagon went past, calling and waving, and Dickon heard Rosa's voice answering from the back of the wagon.

"We go now to wine festival at Orthez," Sebastien told him. "Make good money there. Afterwards to mountains, and home. Do much work." He smiled. "Is good, no? You teach bear to dance."

Dickon nodded, watching the long, straight road

through the horse's ears, and remembering how the Bear Catcher had talked of hot coals under the bear's feet. He would have to find another way.

The next day, and the next, they travelled through the vineyards, and at night Sebastien drew the wagon up beside a stream or a lake, and they made camp for the night. The cub was quiet enough during the day, and seemed to sleep much of the time in the hamper. But in the evening, after it had eaten and drunk, it grew curious and playful, ambling about and exploring the new place they had come to and once trying to climb a tree. Then Dickon would take it through its tricks again, making it sit, and stand, and walk on, while Rosa watched and nodded, saying what a clever Nounou it was.

"Soon we see mountains," Rosa told him on the third evening, as Dickon tied the cub to the wheel of the wagon. "Tomorrow, maybe. Nounou will be glad then." She squatted down beside him. Sometimes, now, the cub let her stroke its head. "Nounou... Nounou..." she said softly, and then looked up at Dickon. "Cub try to run away, you think? Bite through rope, perhaps?"

"I was thinking the same thing," Dickon nodded.

Since they arrived in France the cub seemed to chew at whatever was nearby. It could easily gnaw through the rope during the night. He still had the leather nose strap, but he hadn't put it on since they left England.

"From now on I'll put the muzzle on at night," he said. "To make certain."

By the afternoon of the next day a line of mountains appeared in the distance, under the blue haze of the sky. Rosa pointed excitedly towards them.

"See!" she cried. "Soon we shall be at home, two days, three days maybe."

"First we go to Orthez," Sebastien said. "Good money there!"

By the evening of the following day they were within sight of the town. It stood on a hill, at the foot of the mountain range, a cluster of roofs and a church tower, pink and white under the setting sun. They made camp early that evening, and Dickon felt a new sense of excitement in the air.

"Now you see how we work," Sebastien told him, as Marie and Bruno fixed the tight-rope between the wagon and a nearby tree. Rosa had already disappeared inside the wagon to change out of her long skirt and into the hose she had been wearing when he saw her outside the Bear Garden. "Tomorrow," Sebastien went on, "you play music for us, maybe. Make people look as we go by."

"If you want," Dickon nodded, pleased to be asked to do something, just as though he really was part of the troupe now.

"And Nounou?" Rosa asked, sticking her head out from between the canvas flaps on the back of the wagon.

"I could lead the cub into town," Dickon said eagerly.

But Sebastien shook his head.

"Not yet," he said. "More work first."

Seeing that he would be in the way once they started practising, Dickon took the cub over to a tree a little distance away and, tying it to the trunk, he sat down beside it and began to play over some of his tunes for the following day. Often he stopped to stare at Rosa, who was balancing on the tight-rope, and then at Bruno and Sebastien and Marie, who were trying out their tumbling act and juggling with the painted wooden skittles he had seen propped up inside the wagon. But it was Rosa he watched the most. She was so light, so agile, she seemed to move through the air like thistle-down.

The next morning they set off early, before the sun was up, and had travelled for two hours before they stopped for breakfast. Orthez had seemed close the night before, but Sebastien told Dickon they would not be there until noon.

"Eat plenty," Sebastien said, pointing to the eggs and bread that Marie had been getting ready.

"Papa means that we eat no more till afterwards," Rosa explained. "After..." She frowned.

"After your performance," Dickon nodded.

"Yes. Then eat big meal at Inn. Hubert is friends with Papa."

After breakfast was finished and they were back on the wagon again, no one spoke much. Dickon was sitting between Sebastien and Bruno, but as they reached the outskirts of the town Sebastien handed the reins to Bruno and, jumping down from the wagon, he walked along beside them, waving to the people they passed and telling them to come to the square and see them perform. After a while he signalled to Dickon to begin playing, and taking the flute from inside his jerkin, Dickon put it to his lips and began to play the most cheerful music he knew. Soon people were stopping to stare as they passed, pointing towards Sebastien in his red and yellow tumbler's clothes, and laughing as he swept off his striped hat with the bells on it and bowed low to them. Rosa had jumped off the wagon and ran along beside him, and by the time they reached the market

172

square and Bruno had drawn up the wagon a small crowd was following them.

"Play!" Sebastien nodded to Dickon. "Play more. . ." And while he and Bruno set up their stage, Dickon played on. Drawn by the sound of the music, more and more people came towards them until, by the time everything was ready, a large crowd had gathered around the wagon.

Then Sebastien signalled to Dickon to stop. Bringing the tune to an end with a flourish, Dickon put down the flute. For a moment there was silence, and then to his surprise he heard a cheer from somewhere in the crowd, and the people began to clap.

"You see, they like your music," Rosa said, reaching up and taking his hand. "Now you must bow." And Dickon, feeling his cheeks begin to flame, stood up on the front of the wagon and gave a low bow.

It was when he straightened up that he saw the man: a tall figure at the back of the crowd, dressed all in furs, although the midday sun shone warmly. He was staring intently at Dickon and for an instant their eyes met across the heads of the people. Then, with a slight smile and a nod, the tall man turned away and moved into a side street.

And in that moment Dickon felt a cold finger of fear laid against his heart. For the man dressed all in furs was the Bear Catcher.

Chapter Eleven

*T*ime comes when I am back on the mountainside again, I and the little beast with two legs, and it is well with us. Now I can smell the trees and the grasses and there are good things to eat. I can dig for them in the ground, or fish for them in the mountain stream. The little beast with two legs brings me other food, and when the dark time comes his nest is close to mine. When the light time comes again, we leave the cave and go out into the meadow. Then I may not go beyond the rope's end, and when the little beast talks to me in his language I must do as he bids me ... sit, stand, walk. All this I do for him.

Only sometimes I smell my own mountain, not far off, over this rock, over that ridge, and it is strong in me to go there. But this the little beast does not understand, for though wise in the ways of men he cannot speak my language. Still I do as he bids me, for he is gentle and I will stay with him.

Time comes when there is danger on the mountain-side. The smell of it is all around me. Then I remember the time of blood and whips. I try to tell the little beast that there is danger, but he cannot understand, he does not snuff the air, he cannot smell it as I can. He cannot tell when the danger is near, nor when it has gone away again.

Time comes when the winter wind blows from the mountains. I smell it and know that the meadow is safe again for the little beast, the little she-beast and me.

Dickon didn't see the Bear Catcher again in Orthez, although he looked for him amongst the crowd in the market square. But he had vanished as mysteriously as he had come, and there was no sign of him when they drove out two days later.

All the same, he could not quite forget him. As the golden autumn turned towards winter, and early morning mists wrapped the mountain valley in a clinging, white mantle, he sometimes imagined in those first days that he could hear whistling, soft and low, amongst the dripping trees when Sebastien took them to the woods to gather mushrooms. Then, while Rosa dashed about, searching under the trees for the big brown and orange caps, Dickon would stand still, listening, and sometimes the cub, too, would look up from its rooting among the carpet of dead leaves, and snuff the air as though it scented some kind of danger. Or he would be in the meadow with Rosa and the cub, and the thought of the Bear Catcher's tall, fur clad figure would come unbidden to his mind. He would turn round, then, scanning the rocks and trees that bordered the meadow, half expecting to see him standing there, watching him as he had done that day in Orthez.

"What are you looking at?" Rosa asked him once, a puzzled expression on her face. "There is no one there."

Dickon, thinking she would laugh at him if he told her, passed it off with a shrug, making up some story about a bird he had seen. But there were times, too, in those first days when the cub grew restless and ill at ease, so that Dickon had to coax it to work, until at last it would stop what it was doing, and stand still, alert and watchful, turning first this way and then that, its nose quivering, as though it scented some kind of danger.

"I think Nounou smells another bear," Rosa said. "Or maybe it is wolves."

Dickon stared towards the distant peaks, a great way off, where Sebastien had told him the wolves lived and hunted.

"Do the wolves come down to the valley?" he asked.

Rosa shook her head.

"Only when the snow is deep on the ground," she said.

But there was no snow now, just warm autumn sunshine, and the leaves of the forest turning scarlet and gold. Nothing to be afraid of, he told himself. They were safe enough here, he and the cub. No one ever came up the path, unless it was Bruno and Marie who lived in their own house further down the hill, or the charcoal burners returning from the village to their hut, deep in the woods. The Bear Catcher must be a hundred leagues away by now, Dickon thought. Probably he would never see him again.

So he said nothing to Rosa, nor to Sebastien and as the days slipped past and the cub grew more content he forgot about the Bear Catcher.

Each day Nounou's pelt seemed to grow thicker and more alive, and the flesh filled out over his ribs. He was getting stronger too, strong enough to push Dickon over, though he meant him no harm. The day after they arrived, Sebastien had given Dickon a great coil of rope, long enough to go twice round the little wooden house, and now the cub could wander at will, far down the meadow. After the day's work was done, Dickon and Rosa would sit, watching it dig with long claws amongst the grasses and under the roots of trees for the things it liked to eat. Sometimes, then, Dickon would feel a tug on the rope, and looking up he would see the cub's face turned towards him, as though questioning why it could go no further. It would shake its head in puzzlement and, sitting down with a sigh, would stay some time, snuffing the air and gazing far off to the ridges of the mountains where the first snow had already fallen. Then Dickon felt sad, for he knew that no matter how long the rope was, it could never be long enough.

"Why does Nounou go sniff ... sniff ... all the time?" Rosa asked one afternoon, as they sat at the top of the meadow.

"Maybe bears smell what we see," Dickon said. "That's what I think anyway."

Rosa cupped her chin in her hands, thinking it over.

"You mean that Nounou's nose is like our eyes?" she said, after a moment. Dickon nodded, watching the cub which still sat at the bottom of the meadow, nose pointing towards the distant ridge of mountains, snout moving gently back and forth.

"Perhaps it smells its home," he said, after a moment. Rosa turned quickly and looked at him.

"Nounou's home is here with us," she said fiercely.

"I know," Dickon nodded. "Now. But before. . ."

"Before?" She frowned.

"Before Nounou was brought to England," Dickon said, running the rope through his hands as the thought of the Bear Catcher came unbidden to his mind. Rosa chewed on a bit of grass, watching him, and for a while neither of them said anything. The sun had dropped behind the mountain and it was growing cold. Dickon shivered.

"You are sad today, I think," Rosa said gently, putting her hand on his arm. "You do not like to be here with Papa and me? You like to go back to England, maybe?" She gave him a searching look.

"No," Dickon said. "No, you don't understand. I like it here. In truth I do."

He wanted to explain that if it wasn't for her he would probably be begging in the streets of London with Nounou at his heels. All at once he wanted to tell her about the Bear Catcher, too, and about how the rope would never be long enough. He wanted to tell her many things. But it was too difficult. One day he would tell her everything, but not now.

"It's getting cold," he frowned. "And it's time for Nounou's supper."

He jumped up quickly and began to haul at the rope, and the cub, feeling the tug, turned and came slowly up the meadow towards them.

And so the days slipped past until Christmastide. It was cold in the mountain valley now, and the cub had begun to sleep longer, curled up in the barn in a great heap of straw, so that there was nothing to be seen but the tip of his snout. Sebastien told Dickon that it was the way with some beasts to while away the coldest part of the year in sleep.

"In the spring your Nounou will come out again," he said. "Then you teach the cub to dance, yes?"

Dickon nodded, though his heart sank at Sebastien's words, for try as he might he had so far not found a way to make the cub lift its feet. It would come now, when Dickon called, stand, and sit and even roll over and play dead; it had learnt to walk well with the rope, and no longer tugged and fought, so that sometimes Dickon would see Sebastien give a satisfied nod as he watched Dickon putting the cub through its paces. But still Nounou would not dance. He was beginning to wonder if the cub would ever learn. But somehow, Dickon thought, he must contrive to keep his part of the bargain they had made. Somehow when spring came he must teach the bear cub to dance.

The days were growing shorter now, and the nights were longer and colder, and while the cub slept on, Dickon and Rosa spent much of their time around the little wooden house. In the evenings they sat by the fire, and with Rosa perched on the three-legged stool at his feet, Sebastien would tell stories of old times, or sing the songs of the mountains. And pulling out his flute, Dickon would play the songs as Sebastien sang them, so that before long he had learnt many new tunes.

They saw little of Bruno and Marie during that time, except when Bruno walked up the valley to talk to Sebastien and make plans for the coming year. Dickon always felt uncomfortable when Bruno came. He seldom smiled or laughed, as Sebastien did, and apart from a brief nod in Dickon's direction when he arrived, he paid him no further attention. Rosa seemed to feel uneasy with him, too, for whenever his tall figure appeared in the doorway, stooping so as not to bang his head, she would grow silent, staying close to Sebastien or else, grabbing Dickon's hand, would drag him off to chop firewood, or see to the cub. Once or twice Dickon had caught a brooding, angry look on Bruno's face as he watched them together.

"Bruno doesn't like me," he said to Rosa one day as they were feeding the fowls while Bruno and Sebastien talked by the fire.

"You?" She gave him a quick, surprised look and then shook her head. "No, 'tis not you."

"What then?" Dickon frowned.

"'Tis Bruno," she said. "That's the way he is." She frowned, her dark eyebrows drawn together into a line. "Always trying to tell Papa what to do, when Papa is in charge."

"I don't think he wants me or the bear cub to be here," Dickon said slowly. But Rosa shook her head again.

"Bruno is for Bruno," she said. "That's all. You will see ... next year, when Nounou can dance and you play your flute ... then we will make a lot of money, and Bruno will be happy. Besides," she went on fiercely, "I like you, and Papa likes you. You are one of us now. You are my brother."

She had grown a little pink. Dickon could feel the flush beginning to creep up his own cheeks as he scattered the last of the grain for the fowls that pecked at their feet.

It was true, he thought. Rosa had become like a

sister to him. Not the same as Ann, of course, for no one could ever take her place. But Ann was older than him, and had always looked after him. With Rosa he felt an equal, for they were the same age and, although a maid, she was as fearless as any boy and never moped or sulked the way some did.

"Since you have no mother and I have no father, we had best be brother and sister and stick together," Dickon said gruffly.

"You feel that, too," she said in a low voice. "I knew you did! Now we must swear a blood bond," she added, jumping off the wall and beginning to unpin the clasp that held her cloak. "Then we will truly be brother and sister."

And holding out her hand, she jabbed the pin fearlessly into her middle finger until a drop of blood spurted out.

"This was my mother's brooch," she said. "That makes it a true bond, doesn't it?" She handed Dickon the brooch. "Now it's your turn," she said.

Seeing the solemn look on her face, Dickon took the brooch and stuck the pin into his finger as she had done. Rosa nodded when she saw the bead of crimson blood, and put her hand against his so that their fingers were touching. When they had both vowed to be true brother and sister to one another,

Rosa gave a quick nod, and pinned the brooch back on her cloak.

There had been a fall of snow in the night, and being by then rather too full of feelings that didn't go well into words they began to pelt each other with snowballs.

The next day was Christmas Eve. As soon as the noonday meal was over Sebastien harnessed the horse, and telling them both to jump up on to the wagon, set off down the mountain to buy food for the Christmas feast. Rosa's face was serious as she stood beside Sebastien in the crowded market, helping to choose the plumpest goose and the finest chestnuts and sweet dried apricots, onions and herbs. The stalls were piled high with good things – apples and walnuts, dates from Africa and bright, glowing oranges, sweet almonds and raisins, strings of sausages and baskets of eggs and roasted hams, chestnuts in syrup and candied fruits and sugared cakes and jars of honey, so that soon their basket was laden too heavily for Rosa to carry, and with a laugh Sebastien picked it up and set it upon his shoulder. Then there were gifts to be bought for Marie and Bruno, who were coming to share the feast, and later, as the church bell tolled out for eleven o'clock, they joined the people who jostled inside for the Christmas Mass. Standing shoulder to shoulder with Rosa and Sebastien in the dark, candlelit church, Dickon thought of Ann and Jacob, so far away from him in London, and felt a lump come to his throat.

Afterwards, driving back to the mountain valley under the stars, Rosa slipped her arm through his.

"They say that on Christmas Eve all the animals can talk," she said. "Perhaps it's true, perhaps Nounou will be able to speak to us tonight."

Dickon half believed her, for it was a night made for the old stories. But when they crept into the barn, the cub was as fast asleep as ever, and said not a word.

With Christmas over, work began in earnest. There were new routines to be practised, new costumes to be made, and the wagon itself to be readied for the day when they set off. One of the shafts was cracking, and Sebastien must fashion a new one. Once they left the mountain valley they would spend the spring and summer on the road, Rosa told Dickon, not returning until autumn.

Bruno and Marie walked over almost every day now, and for as long as the light lasted the four of them worked on their act. Dickon was needed too, then, and while the cub slept on in the barn, and the snow lay deep on the ground, he practised with them, playing the tunes that Sebastien had picked out to accompany their routines. There was a serious businesslike air about the place now; watching them at work each day, Dickon soon saw that although Sebastien was the leader of the troupe, Bruno was the better acrobat. Sebastien worked with a smile, encouraging everyone; with Bruno it was different. If things did not go as he wanted, he would scowl and mutter, and often Dickon, who could understand most of what was said by then, saw Rosa flush at the sharpness of his criticism.

"He is so hard on you," he said to her one day after Bruno and Marie had gone home and they were fetching more wood from the log pile. "It's unkind ... you're just as good as he is."

Rosa shook her head.

"Bruno is the best acrobat in all France," she said, her dark eyes serious. "I will never be one half as good as he is."

"Don't you mind when he chides you?" Dickon asked. She stood still for a moment, a log in each hand.

"But that is how I learn," she said. "Why should I mind? And he is always right, you know."

Dickon bit his lip and said no more.

One afternoon about a week later, when Bruno

and Marie had been practising a new part of their routine, Sebastien asked Dickon to fetch his flute and try out some music with them.

"The gavotte you were playing yesterday evening," he said.

Perched on the three-legged stool, Dickon began to play.

But Bruno, so sure footed as a rule, must have made a wrong move, for an instant later there was a thump and Dickon saw Marie land heavily on the floor.

"Devil take it," Bruno exclaimed. "Now see what you've made me do."

"Me?" Marie retorted, rubbing her back. "It was you, you clumsy oaf, you dropped me!"

"Don't blame me," Bruno told her roughly. "It's not my fault. It's that crazy boy over there. Music, music, all the time. I can't concentrate. Why don't you tell him to stop?" he went on, turning furiously on Sebastien.

"Let's try it once more without the music then," Sebastien said gently, gesturing to Dickon to stop.

"I don't know why we need him anyway," Bruno muttered. "Instead of watching us, the people will be listening to him."

"You are wrong, Bruno," Sebastien said quietly.

"We have needed a musician for some time now. We agreed – you remember. And you will see ... the act will go better with Dickon and the bear cub."

"The bear cub! Huh! That's a joke!" Bruno said, throwing back his head. "A great joke! We only took the boy on because of the bear, and all the brute does is sleep. Can it dance yet? I ask you, can it dance? Because if it can I haven't seen it."

Dickon felt the crimson flush creeping over his face and saw Rosa open her mouth to protest. But Sebastien put his hand quickly on her shoulder.

"The wind is in an evil direction today," he said drily. "Perhaps we have all worked long enough. Come, let's stop and have a draught of wine to cheer ourselves up. Rosa, fetch the cups."

"And I will help you," Dickon said, sliding off the stool.

Bruno spun round to watch them go, and a startled expression crossed his face.

"Now he will be sorry," Rosa whispered as they went through the door. "He thought you couldn't speak our language, but you understood every word, didn't you?"

"Enough to know that he doesn't want me in the troupe," Dickon said. "But I've known that all along."

"He will be glad in the end," Rosa told him fiercely. "You'll see ... once Nounou has learnt to dance – "

"You keep saying that," Dickon cut in. "But Nounou is still asleep and time is running out, and I'm not sure any longer that I can teach the cub to dance. I thought I could. . ." He broke off with a frown.

"You'll find a way," Rosa told him. "I know you will. When spring comes and Nounou wakes up, you'll find a way."

But Dickon was not so sure.

Later, as Rosa was preparing a dish of eggs for their supper after Bruno and Marie had gone, Sebastien spoke to him.

"You must not mind Bruno," he said, looking up from the harness he was polishing. "He is the best acrobat and juggler in all France, but sometimes his temper is a little warm." Dickon said nothing, but frowned, staring into the flames. "You will see," Sebastien went on after a moment. "Once we are on the road again things will be different."

"That's what Rosa said," Dickon muttered.

"And she is right," Sebastien nodded. "When Bruno is not working he broods and becomes bad tempered. He cannot help himself. As soon as he has an audience and hears some applause again, he will be all smiles. Rosa understands that."

Dickon leaned forward to throw another log on to the fire and remembered the day in Orthez when he had played his flute, and how good he had felt to hear the people clapping him.

"Another few weeks and we shall be on the road," Sebastien went on. "Then we shall travel and work all summer ... and you, Dickon, you will be one of us. Will you like that, do you think?"

"My father travelled, too," Dickon said. "He was a merchant and was often from home."

"Aye, so I heard," Sebastien nodded. "Travelling is in your blood, maybe."

"But I like it here as well," Dickon said. "With you and Rosa." And then, taking up a stick, he poked suddenly at the fire.

He wanted to thank Sebastien for rescuing him and the cub and bringing them both here. He wanted to tell him how hard he would work, and that somehow he would teach the cub to dance, and that this was the happiest he had been since before his father died. But none of the right words would come, so he just went on poking the fire and making the sparks fly up the chimney in a golden shower, until Sebastien leant forward and put a hand on his shoulder.

191

"Enough," he said. "No need to beat the fire to death. I understand. And when you go to bed tonight, tell that bear cub of yours that it's time to wake up. Spring is coming, and there's work to be done."

Sebastien was right. Three days later Dickon woke to hear rain on the barn roof. The cub had heard it too; from below came the sound of snuffling as Nounou burrowed out of the pile of straw.

Spring had come, and once having arrived it meant to stay. The rain stopped, the sun came out, the grass and flowers started to push up through the earth, and within a week the mountain valley was carpeted with colours, and the cub, ravenous after its long sleep, must needs eat all day to make up for lost time.

"Nounou, Nounou, how thin you are!" Rosa exclaimed anxiously.

"So would you be if you'd eaten nothing for two months," Dickon grinned, watching the cub roll in the grass, eat, roll again, and then stagger the full length of the rope as it rediscovered the delights of the meadow once again. Best of all, it was as though the two month sleep had seemed no longer to the cub than a single night, for Dickon discovered to his delight that it remembered all it had been taught.

192

The time had come to begin the dancing lessons in earnest.

He started by tapping each of the cub's feet in turn, which made it stare curiously at first and then grunt with annoyance. Seeing that it was no use, Dickon fetched twine and tied it to each of the cub's legs, to see if he could persuade it to lift its feet that way. But it stood fast and would not budge.

"Honey!" Rosa suggested, running to fetch the precious jar from the store cupboard. Dickon spread it on to a plank of wood, and urged the cub forward until he was standing on it.

"Now he will lift his feet," Rosa nodded, watching from a little way away. But with a grunt of delight the cub sidled off the plank and no more work was done that afternoon as it was too busy licking up the honey until the last morsel had gone.

Sometimes it grew surly, and would stop, shake its head, and with a low growl snuff the air, and then begin padding restlessly to and fro, rolling its eyes this way and that, and refusing to do as it was told. Dickon was growing downhearted.

"What you need is a bed of hot coals," Bruno said one day, watching his efforts from beyond the wall. "He'd soon lift his feet for them."

They were the very same words the Bear

Catcher had used, that first day at the Bear Garden, and for a crazy moment when Dickon looked up he half expected to see the Bear Catcher himself standing there instead of Bruno. He blinked, burying his fingers deeply into the cub's thick pelt, and for a moment could say nothing. It was Rosa who spoke.

"But that would hurt his feet," she exclaimed. "It would be cruel."

"So..." Bruno shrugged. "It's only a dumb beast."

"Nounou saved Dickon's life," Rosa retorted hotly. "He is a special bear cub."

"Have it your own way," Bruno said shortly. "But there's not much money to be made out of a dancing bear that won't dance."

"Perhaps he is right," Dickon said, watching Bruno walk off down the path, whistling as he went. "Perhaps there is no other way..." Rosa stared at him, aghast.

"But you wouldn't – would you?"

"Of course not," Dickon said, putting his arm around the cub's neck. "But we've tried everything I can think of, and it's no use." He sighed and shook his head. "I thought I could do it, but I can't."

The mournful sound of whistling still floated up

to them from further down the valley, seeming to weave a circle around them. Dickon shivered.

"You mustn't give up," Rosa said, leaning forward. "There's still time. We'll think of something. Bad Nounou," she went on, turning to the cub and starting to lecture it, her finger wagging.

"No," Dickon said, shaking his head. "That's not true. I don't believe that Nounou sees the point of it, that's all."

And the cub, looking from one to the other of them, shook its head as though it understood every word.

The next day Sebastien harnessed the mare and, leaving Dickon in charge, set off with Rosa to buy provisions. Dickon watched them go, knowing that today might be his last chance to teach the cub to dance. They would be alone together all day and deep into the evening for Sebastien had said that he and Rosa would eat supper with Bruno and Marie and would not return until after dark. Today, Dickon thought, he must find a way, for the following week they would be leaving the valley. He was just taking the cub to the meadow, when he saw Rosa running up the hill towards him, waving and calling.

"What's happened?" he asked, frowning, as she came closer.

"Nothing, but I had an idea," she panted. "About Nounou. I came to tell you."

"But you wanted to go with Sebastien," Dickon frowned.

"I know, but this is more important." She did a couple of forward flips and landed near him. "Water," she said.

"Water?" Dickon said blankly.

"Water," she nodded, her cheeks pink. "If we throw a cup of water on to each paw in turn, maybe..."

"It might work," Dickon said slowly. And then, more eagerly. "Suppose we tie him to the post..." Rosa nodded.

"And it won't hurt," she said.

Dickon tethered the cub to the post that Sebastien had put up in the meadow, while Rosa fetched a bucket of water from the well.

Dickon hadn't expected that it would work, but to his surprise, as soon as he threw the first cup of ice cold water on to Nounou's foot, the shock of it made him lift his paw from the ground for a moment.

They grinned at each other.

"Now the other one," Rosa said.

All afternoon they worked; backwards and forwards Rosa ran to the well to fetch pail after pail of water, until the shadows lengthened across the meadow and the sun began to slip behind the rim of the mountains.

"Up," Rosa cried, each time she threw the water, and each time Dickon played the same three quick notes on his flute.

"Up, Nounou, up!"

At last the cub grew tired and would do no more. But it didn't matter. There would be tomorrow and the day after. There would be many tomorrows.

"You did it!" Dickon cried. "You found the way." And seizing her hands he whirled her round and round the meadow in a mad dance, faster and faster, until they both collapsed in a breathless heap amongst the gold of the buttercups and celandine. The cub, too, sensing that the day's work was over, was rolling in the grass, all four paws in the air.

Suddenly it reared up again, snuffing the air and growling.

Dickon frowned uneasily, and looked round. But the valley was silent, except for the chattering alarm call of a blackbird beyond the meadow.

"Nounou is tired," Rosa said, jumping off the wall. "Never mind, Nounou, good Nounou, I have a sugared loaf for you, a huge one, your favourite."

Dickon gathered up the rope and followed her as

she ran ahead to the house, and came out carrying the loaf, just as he reached the barn.

He was hugely, triumphantly glad, and laughing at the way she danced about, waving the loaf in front of the cub's nose. They had almost reached the barn door, when it suddenly stopped.

"It's your favourite," Rosa teased, backing towards the open door. "Just a few steps more, then you shall have it ... good Nounou ... dear Nounou..."

And then Dickon stopped laughing. For an arm came out from behind the barn door and pulled Rosa inside, and as the cub plunged and snarled in sudden fear, straining at the rope, Dickon saw the glint of the knife.

Chapter Twelve

N ow it is too late to fight, too late to turn and run. For the danger is upon us. It is here ... now ... the time of whips and blood has come again.

We are caged, the little beast, the little she-beast and I. They have their own cage, but it is close to mine. The little beast reaches through the bars when I groan, and puts his hand on my head. He knows that I am sore from the whipping. Then he makes a sound like the wind on the grass, and the salt water runs down his face and falls in drops on to his hands. That means the little beast is sad, as I am. I stay close to him and lick the salt drops from his hands.

Bump, bump, bump ... crack of the whip ... lurch ... rattle, bump ... one day ... two days ... swaying and grinding and climbing, up, up, ever up. In the morning the sun was behind them. Dickon knew that meant they were travelling west. Deeper and deeper into the high mountains they went, where the snow lay in pockets between the boulders and the wind blew sharp and keen.

And as they travelled on the Bear Catcher whistled, hunched over the reins at the front of the wagon, the same dreary tuneless tune, that grated on Dickon's ear.

He shivered and looked across at Rosa. Her eyes were half closed, and she sat quite still, leaning against the side of the cage, her cloak bunched around her and her knees drawn up. He wondered that she could keep so still, hardly moving except when the wagon jolted her from side to side. If only she hadn't come back, he thought, for the hundredth time, his mind running round and round like a crazy, hunted rabbit that hears the dogs. If only she had gone with Sebastien she would be safe now, instead of shut up in the Bear Catcher's wagon, with him and the cub. And she hadn't cried, not once. If she'd cried he could have comforted her.

"What are you thinking about?" he whispered, leaning forward and touching her foot.

"About the act," she said softly, pushing the dark tangle of hair away from her face. "I go through it in my mind, so that I won't forget." Her eyes had a far away look. "I must be perfect for the first time."

Dickon frowned.

"There's not going to be a first time," he said, as gently as he could. "Not now."

But Rosa was smiling.

"Soon," she whispered. "Sebastien will find us very soon. You'll see."

Dickon stared at her. Then he shook his head.

"No!" he said. "No – it's not possible. You mustn't think that. It's been almost two days now."

In front of them the Bear Catcher shifted on his seat and half turned, and Rosa lifted her finger to her lips in warning. Then the mule stumbled, and as the wagon rolled and lurched he gave a curse, and they heard him crack the whip.

"He will never find us," Dickon whispered after a while, when the whistling had begun again. "Look at these mountains, miles and miles of them."

She leant forward swiftly and put her hand across his mouth.

"Don't talk of it now," she told him softly, jerking her head towards the Bear Catcher. "Just believe me. I know he will come."

After a moment Dickon shrugged and turned away. Sebastien would never find them, whatever she thought. It would be like looking for a needle in a haystack. Somehow they would have to plan a way to escape. He leant back against the wooden slats of the cage, and closed his eyes.

It was all his fault, he thought miserably. He should have told Rosa and Sebastien, that very first day in Orthez, when he had seen the Bear Catcher. That was when it began. Ever since then, deep down inside him, he had known the Bear Catcher would come for them, and in those first days, when it was restless, and snuffed the air and growled, the cub had known as well; known that the Bear Catcher was somewhere close by, waiting and watching. After that he had gone away for a while, to make his plans and wait until the spring; until a day when Sebastien wasn't there.

Dickon had felt no surprise, seeing him sidle out of the barn, his arm round Rosa and the knife held at her throat. It had seemed like something that was going to happen for a long time. Only Rosa shouldn't have been there, Dickon thought, frowning, and remembering the look on the Bear Catcher's face. He hadn't expected Rosa.

He opened his eyes and frowned down at the crack between the boards. He could see the road through it as the wagon rumbled on. The Bear Catcher must have come from over the mountain, he thought, creeping down when it started to grow dark, and hiding in the barn. That was the way he had taken them afterwards, scrambling up the steep, narrow path towards the summit and then along the ridge, deep into the forest. If he had come up the valley, he would have seen them in the meadow and known that Rosa was there. And if he had come that way the cub would have sensed the danger, too, long before it did. For the cub had always known when he was near. Dickon realized that now.

And if Rosa had not been there, Dickon thought, if she had gone with Sebastien as she was meant to, it would have looked for all the world as though he had run away and taken the cub with him.

But that part of the plan had gone wrong, and just for a moment the Bear Catcher hadn't known what to do as he stood there with the knife held at Rosa's throat, and his hand over her mouth.

"You're coming with me," he had said. "You and that bear cub of yours." He hadn't said anything about Rosa, not at first.

If he'd been alone, just him and the cub, Dickon thought, he might have tried to run away, or made a fight of it. But Rosa's eyes stared at him, wide and dark, and he saw the knife glint and turn.

"Let her go," he had said, shortening the rope between his hands as the cub growled and bucked.

"She has nothing to do with this. It's me you've come for, isn't it? Me and the cub."

"True enough," he nodded, giving Dickon a long, slow look. And then he had smiled. "Still, 'twill not do to leave the wench behind. She'll spread tales about me, and that would never do. Besides, with my knife at her throat you'll not be tempted to run away, will you?"

"If you leave her here I'll not run away," Dickon said. "I swear it."

" 'Tis no use to argue with me once my mind's set on a thing," the Bear Catcher said. "You should know that by now. I say the wench comes too, and that's an end to it."

Dickon put his hand on the cub's head to try and quieten it, and glanced quickly at Rosa. The Bear Catcher had lowered the knife, and she was wriggling, the sugared loaf still clutched in one hand.

"Only tell me where you're taking us," he said quickly, seeing the Bear Catcher tighten his grip on her.

"Why, a long way from here," he answered. "And now, if you're ready, we'd best be going."

"It will be cold," Dickon said, pointing to Rosa's cloak which had fallen off and lay on the ground. "At least let her pick it up. No harm in that, is there?"

The Bear Catcher gave a grunt and, still holding the knife with one hand, he used the other to pull a length of rope from the pocket of his surcoat, which he tied around Rosa's waist.

"Make haste then," he said. "I would be gone from here. Make haste, I say."

Rosa bent down and picked up the cloak, and as she straightened up again and looked across at Dickon, he saw her eyes blaze for a moment. Then the Bear Catcher gave her a sharp push.

"You lead the beast," he told Dickon. "I will see to her. And remember, the knife is here in my hand."

He had taken them to a cave deep in the woods that first night. He must have been using it while he was watching the valley, for there were cooking pots, and a hammock slung between two rocks. Tied together, back to back and gagged so that they could not talk, neither of them had slept much that night. As for the cub, it was left chained up outside. At dawn, they set off again, and before the sun was up had reached the wagon that stood in a clearing near the road, the mule tethered nearby. It was the same wagon that Dickon had seen that first day at the Bear Garden, and the cub, recognizing it too, had refused to budge when the Bear Catcher tried to lead it inside. That was when he had whipped it for the first time, and Dickon, bound and gagged, could only watch and feel the hatred surge in his heart.

Now, sitting in the wagon, his hand stretched through the slats towards the cub's pelt, he shuddered again as he remembered the cub's howls of pain.

He looked across at Rosa. She had a handful of greyish pebbles in her lap, and sat, clicking them together and running them through her hands. She must have picked them up along the way, he thought, seeing the rays of the setting sun slope through the gaps in the canvas and dance around her fingers.

Soon, he thought, they would have to stop. The mule had been travelling all day. How many miles had they come? he wondered. And if they did manage to escape, how would they ever find the way back?

He looked at Rosa, but her head was turned away from him, and she stared down at the pebbles. Click, click, click. He wished she would say something . . . anything. The clicking stopped for a moment, and then he saw her hand move towards the crack between the planks. The next moment she had pushed one of the pebbles through it, down on to the road. Then, as though nothing had happened, her hand went back to her lap, and she began running the pebbles through her fingers again.

Dickon's heart started to pound. He leant back against the slats and watched her through half-closed eyes. Once she looked up at him, and then down again. Click, click, went the pebbles. Dickon waited until he saw her hand move again. This time there was no doubt about it. He leant quickly forward.

The sudden movement made her jump. For a moment her eyes widened, and she shot a quick glance over her shoulder towards the Bear Catcher. But the whistling hadn't stopped, and his back was still towards them. She smiled at Dickon and put her finger to her lips. For a moment hope blazed inside him.

It wasn't only the pebbles, there was something else, too. He tried to think. Then it came to him. Her cloak. Ever since they had left she'd been pulling at it, to stop it slipping off. He'd never seen her do that before. The brooch ... the brooch that pinned it to her shoulder, the one that had belonged to her mother. He stared across at her, looking at the place where it ought to be. But it wasn't there.

"Outside the barn," she whispered, reading his thoughts.

"When you dropped your cloak?" She nodded.

"Sebastien would know then."

"And the sugared loaf?" Dickon whispered, remembering. She shot another quick look over her shoulder and then nodded.

"But the birds might have eaten that," she breathed. "Stones are better." Her hand moved again. There were only a few pebbles left now.

"You should have told me," Dickon said. "All this time. . ."

"I thought you'd guessed," she said.

There was a chance, Dickon thought. Just a chance. Sebastien would not have been able to see the trail until the next morning, but his eyes were sharp. Dickon remembered how he had noticed things in the forest, the footprints of animals, birds' nests, and tell tale signs that foxes and badgers had passed in the undergrowth. He might be no more than half a day's ride behind them.

They had started to go down hill and it was growing dark inside the wagon. The sun must have dropped behind the mountain. But still the Bear Catcher drove the mule forward. It was as though he meant to reach a certain place that night. Dickon stretched out his hand and took Rosa's, gripping it tightly.

When at last they stopped and the Bear Catcher

pulled them roughly out of the wagon, it was too dark to see much. They seemed to be in a large clearing, and Dickon could hear the sound of rushing water close by. Pushing them ahead of him across the stony ground, the Bear Catcher made for the edge of the clearing where a small cabin stood beside a clump of trees, and threw open the door.

It was pitch dark inside, and a dank smell hung in the air. Outside, from somewhere in the distance, came the eerie sound of howling.

"Wolves!" Dickon muttered.

"Aye," the Bear Catcher answered, fumbling with the tinder box. "They're out hunting tonight." He lit the lantern and set it upon the ground, and his pack beside it. "No time to be running away, I'd say," he added, looking from one to the other of them. "You'd best stay in here where it's snug while I see to the mule."

"The cub needs food and water," Dickon said.

"The cub can stay where it is till morning," he answered. "Make yourselves useful and light a fire." And pointing towards the pile of kindling stacked in the corner, he went out.

As soon as he had gone, Dickon turned to Rosa.

"Listen..." he began. But she grabbed his arm and shook her head.

"Not now," she whispered. "Not safe. Do as he says."

The Bear Catcher was whistling when he came back, and seemed to be pleased with himself. He squatted down beside the fire, which was burning brightly by then and, pulling his pack towards him, took out biscuit and strips of hard, salted meat, which he shared between the three of them. To this he added a couple of onions, which he took from his pocket, and after peeling and quartering them he speared a piece on the point of his knife and passed it to Dickon. Remembering how the knife had been at Rosa's throat, Dickon shook his head. The Bear Catcher chuckled, but said nothing.

Hungry though he was, and thirsty too, Dickon could eat little. The meat tasted rancid, and the biscuit stuck to the roof of his mouth. Rosa crumbled the biscuit in her lap, taking nibbles of it now and then, and stared into the fire. Apart from the sound of the Bear Catcher crunching his onions, there was silence. Dickon thought of the cub, outside in the dark and cold.

When he had finished eating, the Bear Catcher set a can of water on the fire, and reaching into one of his pockets pulled out some herbs, which he crumbled into it, adding the last of the onion. Before long, steam rose from the can, and a pungent smell filled the cabin. Fetching a pair of pewter cups from the shelf in the corner he poured some of the liquid into each and handed one of them to Dickon.

"You'll not mind sharing, I fancy," he chuckled. "Seeing as you're such close companions." He looked at them steadily over the rim of his cup, and then stirred the fire with his foot. "Cosy like, ain't it," he said. "Just the three of us, and no one else for a hundred leagues or more – not forgetting the wolves, of course."

The stuff had warmed Dickon's insides and tasted better than he had expected. He took a few more sips and passed the cup to Rosa, nodding to her to drink too.

Then he looked through the smoke at the Bear Catcher.

"How long do you mean to keep us here?" he asked. "It's been three days now."

The Bear Catcher chuckled, and took a swig from his cup. Then he leaned forward.

"Catched you, didn't I?" he nodded. "Catching things is my trade you see. And once catched, I don't let them go – except for a profit that is. I've got plans for you. And that cub of yours." For a moment his gaze rested on Rosa. "Pity about the wench," he said. "Speaks our language, does she?"

"Of course I do," Rosa said scornfully. "And I understand everything you say."

"Aye, I thought as much," the Bear Catcher nodded. "Not that you've talked much. But that's just the way I like it." He turned to Dickon again. "The wench is not important," he said, leaning forward. "It's you I want. Wanted you ever since that day at the Bear Garden, when I saw how the cub came to you. You remember that day, don't you?"

Dickon nodded.

"Aye, of course you do." He took a swig from his cup, and wiped his sleeve across his mouth. "Made up my mind then and there I did," he went on. " 'That's one I'd like to catch for myself,' I thought. 'That's one I could put to good use.' " He chuckled. "Fair pining for you, I was. I'd made up my mind to come back for you next season," he said, nodding his head. "Quite decided on that I was, for I says to myself, Bear Catcher, I says, that boy could be worth a sack of gold to you, seeing the way he was with that cub. And the thought grew and grew in me," he went on, turning the cup slowly in his hands, and smiling lazily at Dickon through the smoke. "I couldn't believe my luck when I saw you in Orthez.

For now, thinks I to myself, I have him within my grasp. Playing the flute you were. And you saw me, too, didn't you?"

Dickon nodded, and felt Rosa turn and look at him.

"Aye, I knew you had done. Got your flute with you now, have you? We could have a tune maybe."

"I don't think I feel like playing tonight," Dickon said.

"Ah well, never mind. There'll be other nights. Plenty of them." He was silent for a while. Then he leaned forward. "Only one thing bothered me that day in Orthez . . . where was the cub? But I found out soon enough."

"You followed us, didn't you?" Dickon said.

"Aye, and watched you, too. Saw how you taught the cub to do your will, out there in the meadow. Made me want you all the more." He took another gulp of the liquid and refilled his cup. "All I had to do was wait for the right moment," he went on. "I laid my plans, rested up through the winter and here we are." For a moment he was silent. Then he leaned forward and smiled. "You knew I'd come for you, didn't you?"

Dickon thought of the sunlit meadow, and of the cub rolling in the grass while he and Rosa sat on the wall, watching. He swallowed hard and shook his head.

"Aye, you knew," the Bear Catcher nodded. "I told you, didn't I? That day at the Bear Garden … born under the same star we were, I said. Well, now you belong to me, just like I planned it. And you're going to work for me – you and the bear cub." His voice was gentle now and he smiled softly.

"Belong? To you?" Dickon cried out. "No, that's not true. I belong to no one. And nor does the bear cub. Why have you brought us here?"

He felt Rosa stir beside him.

"Don't you understand, Dickon?" she said. He turned wildly and stared at her. "You're going to help him to trap bears," she said. "You and Nounou. That's the work he wants you to do for him."

Chapter Thirteen

Rosa's words seemed to echo inside his head. He had known, and yet not known. Even now he didn't quite believe it.

"No," he said, shaking his head and frowning as he turned to look at her. "No . . . that can't be right."

"It is the truth," Rosa said sadly. "I know, Dickon. I've heard it in the village." She looked across at the Bear Catcher who was watching them through the smoke. "You make the tame bear to be a trap, don't you?"

"Aye, a decoy," he nodded.

"That way he won't have to dig the bears out of the ground," she explained. "They smell the tame bear and come to see."

So he was to help him do that . . . to trap more bears . . . to sell them into slavery as his cub had been sold. But he had rescued the cub from all that, he thought. He had brought it here, to the mountains,

where it was happy. And now it was all to begin again
... like a circle that has no ending.

"No," he said. He looked up at the Bear Catcher.
"No. 'Tis cruel," he said. "Horrible... I want no
part of it."

"Tender hearted, ain't you?" the Bear Catcher
smiled. "That's why you couldn't teach the cub to
dance," he went on, pointing a stubby finger at
Dickon. "Hot coals I said – remember? But you'd
not heed me."

"I had no need of hot coals," Dickon flashed.

"Oh," said the Bear Catcher, "so you found
another way, did you?"

"As a matter of fact, we did," Dickon said, and
shot a quick glance at Rosa. For an instant as their
eyes met he saw a ghost of a smile on her face. Then
the Bear Catcher chuckled.

"If 'tis true ... that makes you more valuable than
ever," he said. "And I daresay you'll run my way
soon enough in this, once you've thought things
over. Like I said, you and I were born under the
same star."

Dickon shook his head, and the anger welled up
inside him.

"I am not the same as you," he said, taking a deep
breath. "And I never will be. I think that what you

do is the worst of all. If it wasn't for you," he went on, his voice rising, "my cub would still be free on the mountain, and there would be no bears to fight in the bear pits, or dance in the streets come to that. And if you want me to help you catch more bears, so that they can be whipped and tormented too ... well ... I won't do it. You can whip me each day for a year if you've a mind to ... but I still won't do it."

In the silence that followed he felt Rosa's hand reach out and take his, and saw the glad look she gave him.

The Bear Catcher stirred the fire with his foot.

"Brave words," he said. "And a pretty speech. Still, there's more than one way to stuff a cat with butter."

He didn't speak for a while after that, but his gaze shifted to Rosa. For a long moment he watched her, turning and turning the cup between his hands, until Dickon felt her shiver and draw closer to him.

" 'Tis a pity about the wench," he said at last, setting the cup carefully down on the ground. "I never meant to have her along. It kind of spoils things, don't you think?"

"If you hurt her..." Dickon began.

"Aye, you'd not like that, would you?" he said softly, his eyes turning to Dickon. "You'd not be pleased if I had to take the whip to her, now, would you?"

Dickon gripped Rosa's hand more tightly.

"If you touch her – "

"I haven't said I will, mind," the Bear Catcher cut in.

"But if you do – "

He leant forward suddenly, pointing a finger at Dickon again.

"And if you give over being so cross-grained and awkward with me, maybe I shan't have to," he said. "So you see . . . it's up to you now, isn't it?"

"What do you mean?" Dickon frowned.

"Why, just this," he said. "If you do as you're bid, and willing like, well then I'm prepared to take her along with us. I'll not use the whip on her, I give you my word on that, nor leave her for the wolves to take, like I was thinking of. More than that," he added. "Since this is no life for a wench, I'll drop her off at the first village we come to, in a month's time, safe and sound, and she can go home to her papa. Meantime, she can keep house for us. Now I can't say fairer than that, can I?"

There was a gleam in his eye as he watched them, and his mouth had twisted into a cruel smile.

Dickon looked at Rosa. By the light of the fire he saw that she had grown as pale as ashes at the mention of the wolves, although her eyes were as defiant as ever. If Sebastien came it wouldn't be tonight, Dickon thought. And by the time he arrived, it might be too late. He swallowed. For the present they would have to do as the Bear Catcher said. As though reading his mind, Rosa nodded her head in silent agreement.

"Well?" said the Bear Catcher, looking from one to the other of them. "What do you say?"

"I'll do what you say," Dickon said emptily. "Just so long as you don't harm Rosa."

"And willing like?"

"Yes ... and willing." The words were hard to say.

"That's better," the Bear Catcher nodded triumphantly. "Now that's what I call a fair bargain." And then, apparently satisfied, he gave a mighty yawn. "Time for bed, I'm thinking. Tomorrow morning we rest up. Then we set off on foot. There's a lair I've got my eyes on, up over the next range." He took off his fur hat and laid it down for a pillow. "And don't think of chancing it with the wolves," he added, "for the key's in my pocket ... here." He tapped his chest, and winked knowingly at Dickon.

And then, without another word, rolled himself over on to his side and was soon snoring.

They watched him silently for a few moments, not daring to speak. After a while Rosa squeezed Dickon's hand.

"Do you think you could sleep?" he asked her softly.

"I might," she nodded.

The Bear Catcher snored on.

"I'll stay awake a while," he whispered.

Rosa wrapped her cloak tightly around her, and curled up beside the fire. Before long she, too, was asleep.

Dickon sat, staring into the dying embers and listening to the wolves howling outside. He thought of the cub, alone and bewildered in the darkness, knowing nothing of what lay ahead, and shuddered. In the morning it would be better, he thought. In the morning, perhaps, Sebastien would come.

And then, without him being aware of it, sleep took him.

When he opened his eyes, daylight was filtering through the chinks in the boards. Beside him Rosa still slept, her cheek pillowed in her hand. Dickon started up and looked around him. They were alone beside the burnt out ashes of the fire. The Bear

Catcher had gone. And from outside the cabin he could hear the unmistakable sound of the cub roaring.

He leant over and shook Rosa's shoulder.

"Nounou," he whispered, as her eyes opened. "I must go and see."

She nodded, and then remembering where they were, sat up quickly and looked round, her eyes widening in fear.

"It's all right, he's not here," Dickon said.

"When he comes back we must do whatever he tells us," she whispered. "He mustn't guess."

Dickon nodded, and standing up went over and tried the door. It was latched on the outside. He banged on it with his fist, and after a moment heard footsteps.

The Bear Catcher's good humour had gone, and he glowered at Dickon as he flung open the door.

"The brute roars," he said. "Every wild beast for fifty leagues must have heard. And it has broken its tether."

"Nounou is hungry," Rosa said.

"And thirsty," Dickon nodded. He eyed the whip which the Bear Catcher held in his hand. "Just let me pass and I'll go and see."

"The wench comes too," he said, pulling a length of rope from his pocket.

"Do you think she's going to run away?" Dickon asked. "We made a bargain, remember."

But in truth, as he looked through the open door, he saw that there was nowhere they could run to.

The cabin stood in a grassy clearing, ringed on each side by towering rocks, except for one narrow cleft through which they must have come the night before. Seeing it now, in daylight, Dickon realized what a perfect hiding place it made, for there was no way of escape. On the far side of the clearing, where the rocks rose most steeply, a waterfall tumbled down a chasm in the mountain into a pool, and then on, between two great jagged outcrops of rock, until, far below, it must have reached the valley. The sound of cascading water filled the air, and Dickon could see the spray rise between the twin rocks as the torrent gushed between them.

Rosa had crept up behind him, and as she peered out over his shoulder, he felt her shiver. The Bear Catcher looked at her.

"Aye, you'd not get far in this wilderness," he said. "Nothing but wolves and bears and wild boar for a hundred leagues."

Dickon looked again towards the cleft in the rocks, and wondered whether Sebastien would ever find it.

The way in must be well hidden from the other side. Then the roaring came again.

"Please," he said, "let me go to the cub."

The Bear Catcher gave a grunt, and stood aside to let him pass, and catching hold of Rosa's wrist dragged her after him.

Nounou was a sorry sight indeed. Dickon's heart turned over with pity to see the beautiful pelt all matted and streaked with blood where the Bear Catcher had laid on the whip. But worse than that was the way the cub grovelled and turned inside the cage, panting and roaring by turns, half mad with fear and thirst.

"Oh, Nounou, Nounou!" Rosa cried, and her eyes were burning as she turned on the Bear Catcher. "How could you? Look what you have done!"

"Hold your tongue, wench," he snapped. "I'll take no lectures from you."

Dickon had reached the wagon by then and was about to undo the latch. But as the Bear Catcher and Rosa came nearer, he saw a change come over the cub. It began to growl with a low, threatening sound, its lips curled back from its teeth in a way Dickon had never seen before. He took a step backwards, in spite of himself, but the Bear Catcher stared steadily at it, and showed no sign of fear as he tapped the whip against his leg. The next moment the cub had made a sudden lunge at the side of the cage, its teeth bared savagely.

"What ails the brute?" the Bear Catcher sneered, his gaze not wavering.

"I've never seen it like this before," Dickon said, uneasily.

"They're savage beasts," the Bear Catcher said, "tame them how you will."

Dickon shook his head.

"No," he said, turning and staring at the Bear Catcher who still stood, tapping the whip against his leg. "No. It's you. The cub has not forgotten. You are the one who took it from the mountains. And now you have come back to whip it as you did before."

The man's small eyes shifted towards Dickon.

"'Twill be a sorry thing indeed if I've brought you all this way for nothing," he said in a threatening tone. "I thought you had a way with the beast."

Dickon lifted his chin.

"You know that I have," he said. "You have watched us in the meadow often enough. And that's why you've brought me here, isn't it? So that I can make the bear cub do what you want? But I can do nothing while you stand there with the whip."

The Bear Catcher's eyes flickered, but he said nothing.

"Please," said Dickon. "Just leave us alone."

Suddenly a look of fury spread over the Bear Catcher's face, and grabbing Rosa by the wrist he began to drag her away.

"Rosa must stay here," Dickon said swiftly. "I need her to fetch the water."

"Have it your own way then," he snarled after a moment. "But I shall be watching, and if you don't bring the brute to heel, it will be the worse for you and her."

"He did what you said," Rosa murmured, watching the Bear Catcher walk off towards the cabin. "But Nounou... Oh, Dickon ... poor Nounou!"

"Water," Dickon told her. "Fetch some water. Quick!"

He turned back to the cage. The cub had stopped growling now, and was staring in the direction the Bear Catcher had gone, its snout quivering. Dickon began to talk slowly and quietly to it. At first he was afraid it was too late. The cub didn't even seem to hear him.

"You're thirsty," he said, over and over again. "That's what it is. You want a drink, then everything will be better, you'll see. I'm here now. Everything's going to be all right."

As soon as Rosa came back with the bucket he dipped his hands into it and, holding some water in the palm of his hand, passed it through the bars. Smelling it, the cub tossed its head. Then it sank on to its haunches, slowly turning towards Dickon, as though seeing him for the first time. Only after a while did its snout come forward, and very cautiously it began to lap at the water.

"Now you can have a proper drink from the pool," Dickon said, running his hand over the shaggy brown head and fondling the cub's ears the way it liked.

"And a fish," Rosa said, creeping closer. "Good Nounou ... dear Nounou."

Carefully, Dickon undid the latch of the cage, waving Rosa back as he did so, for he was wary now, and afraid of what the cub might do. The rope that Sebastien had given him had snapped near the collar. Dickon tied it on again, and then began coaxing the cub out of the wagon.

The last three days had weakened it, for it came quietly enough, stopping often to look towards the cabin, until, smelling the water nearby, it quickened its pace.

From a distance the water in the pool had appeared quite still, but as they drew closer Dickon saw how swift and deep it ran towards the gorge, and kept tight hold of the rope around the cub's neck, not allowing it to go too far in. At first it crouched by the edge, drinking without pause. Then, when its thirst was quenched, it made little runs into the water, splashing Dickon and Rosa, and beating at the surface with its paw. There were fish, too, and most of them it ate, swallowing with hungry gulps, but one it missed, striking at it with one paw so that it shot on to the bank and lay gasping. Rosa was beside it in an instant.

"Clever Nounou," she laughed. "This shall be our breakfast." Dickon turned away as she banged its head against a stone, swiftly and without pity.

And all the time the Bear Catcher was watching them. He had moved out of the cabin now, and walked back and forth to the stable, seeing to the mule and strengthening the heavy stakes which were hammered deep into the ground at one side of the clearing. Dickon guessed that he used them to tether the bears after he had trapped them. And as the Bear Catcher watched, the cub was watching him. Not once in all that long morning, as the sun rose over the rim of the mountain and the birds sang in the pine trees, was there a moment when the cub was not aware of where its enemy was, never a moment when it could not smell him.

After a while the Bear Catcher shouted to Dickon that he had set a pan of meal down for the cub beside one of the stakes, and told him to tether it there and not leave the rope too long.

"The cub has caught a fish for us," Rosa called out, holding it up by the tail so that he could see.

"Well, make yourself useful then, if you can," he answered. "Blow up the fire, make some mealy cakes and cook the fish. We have far to go tonight, and a good meal won't come amiss."

When the food was cooked Rosa and Dickon took theirs outside to be near Nounou, and ate with the sun warming their backs. They didn't speak much. They were waiting, listening for the sound of horse's hooves, hoping against hope that Sebastien would come before the Bear Catcher led them deeper into the mountains.

After they had finished eating, Rosa went down to the edge of the pool and began to collect stones, which she gathered together into a little heap, building them carefully one on top of the other. Some she slipped into her pocket. Dickon pretended not to notice, but sat watching Nounou. The cub was quiet now, grooming its pelt with long, even strokes of its tongue, and breaking off every so often to look towards the Bear Catcher who stood nearby in the doorway of the cabin, picking the fishbones from his teeth.

"Which path do we take?" Dickon asked. "Into the mountains. . ."

"Over yonder," he said, jerking his thumb towards the edge of the clearing. Then he belched and looked across at Nounou. "First that beast must have a chain and muzzle. Now you've tamed the brute again so neatly, 'twould never do if it were to run off, would it?" And he levered himself away from the door and went towards the stable.

As soon as he had gone inside Dickon stood up and walked slowly over towards Rosa.

"The path's over there," he said quietly. "On the far side of the clearing. Can you make it out?"

She turned her head.

"I think so," she nodded.

After a while she gathered a few of the pebbles together and started to form an arrow with them on the ground.

Dickon was crouched beside her. The water made a constant rushing sound that filled the clearing. That was why he didn't hear him coming.

It was his shadow that he saw. Then there was a sudden rattle as he dropped the chain he was carrying and pulled out the whip.

"So..." he said softly, looking down at the pebbles. "So that's the game, is it?"

"Game?" Rosa said, looking up, her eyes wide and innocent.

"I knew you were up to something," he nodded, "though you've been so quiet and mouselike all morning. But you don't fool me. This is a sign, isn't it? A nice arrow to say which way we've gone?" And he kicked savagely at the pebbles, scattering them back towards the pool.

"I do not understand," Rosa stammered, jumping up and backing away from him.

"Don't you indeed? Then perhaps you'll understand this," he snarled, beginning to uncoil the whip.

"Don't touch her," Dickon shouted. "She's only playing ... they're stones, that's all."

He tried to get between them, but the Bear Catcher pushed him over. He was still scrambling to his feet when the first cut hit her across the back. She dropped to her knees with a cry of pain that rang round the clearing.

"No!" Dickon cried. "No ... leave her alone!"

230

"Out of my way, lad, or you get the same," he panted. "She's no use to you ... don't you see that? She's just a meddlesome wench."

"No," Dickon cried. "You promised ... and she's done nothing." He caught at his arm. In sudden fury the Bear Catcher turned then on him.

Dickon heard the crack and whine of the lash and felt it land across his shoulders, again and again. He had been beaten before, but never anything like this. He was on his knees now and in his head there was a crying, roaring sound. That wasn't him, he thought. Surely that sound couldn't be him.

Then, as the Bear Catcher coiled the lash to strike again, he heard it as before, and knew it for what it was ... the roar of a raging beast.

Dimly as he saw the Bear Catcher raise his arm, he heard the rush of feet and Rosa's voice crying out to him.

"Dickon ... take care."

He turned, but even before he saw it, he knew. The cub had broken free.

Enormous it seemed ... no longer a cub at all, but a full grown male bear now, and his feet thundered on the ground as he charged across the clearing towards them, shaking the earth with his fury. He came to a stop, and then, rising majestically to his full height, his hackles up and his lips bared in a snarl, came on again, slowly, towards his enemy.

And the Bear Catcher, lifting one arm as if to shield himself, drew back.

"Tell him to keep off," he gasped. "Order him . . . you can do that, can't you?"

"Drop the whip," Dickon cried. "Don't – !"

But already it was too late, for the lash had swung out towards Nounou. It was all the Bear Catcher knew. And the bear came on towards him, step by slow step. Still the Bear Catcher plied the whip as he backed towards the pool, and still the bear advanced.

He was in the water before he realized his danger, gasping and flailing his arms. Dickon watched the whip float swiftly towards the cleft in the rocks . . . so fast it went. And then, with a cry, the Bear Catcher was following it . . . the water was pulling him, faster and faster. He stretched out a hand and tried to catch at one of the rocks.

"Hold on," Dickon cried. "Hold on. . . I'll fetch a rope."

But his fingers were slipping, slipping, and then he gave one last, horrible cry as the water swept him away.

Dickon ran to where the rock jutted out and climbed up. Then, lying full length across it, he peered over. Below him, he could still see the tattered fur coat as it was bounced from one jagged lump of rock to another, now above the torrent, now beneath it, down, down, down, until at last, far below, the Bear Catcher came to rest in another pool, and the water sucked him down for ever.

Rosa was beside him then, and for a while Dickon dared not move from the rock for the shaking of his limbs.

"It was for you," she said. "Nounou did it for you..."

"I know," Dickon nodded, and buried his face in his hands.

After a moment she put her cloak around his shoulders, for he was still shaking.

"We are free," she said, her voice solemn. "Nounou has set us free. And... Oh Dickon, now, I think, we must let Nounou go..."

"Go?"

"Go," she nodded. "Go home..." He gave her a long, wondering look. And Rosa brushed the tears from her eyes and smiled. "That is what you want, isn't it? For Nounou to go home. I think it's what you've always wanted. And look ... look!"

Slowly Dickon turned round to see where she was pointing.

The bear stood in the middle of the clearing on all fours, snuffing the air, swaying its head this way and that way, gazing up towards the distant peaks.

Once Dickon called out . . . once, but no more.

One long, deep groan the bear gave as he turned to gaze at them. Then he shook his head. And slowly, and without looking back again, he walked to the edge of the clearing and began to climb.

Chapter Fourteen

"How did you know?" Dickon asked Rosa much later as they sat on the grass together.

"I could tell," she answered. "A long time ago . . . in the meadow. . . I knew then. The rope was never long enough. You said that, didn't you?"

"Did I?" Dickon frowned.

She nodded.

"I think so. Anyway, I could see for myself that what Nounou really wanted was to be free. Any bear would, I suppose. It's better this way. No more ropes for Nounou now . . . no more begging for titbits or rolling over and playing dead – "

"And no more dancing, either," said Dickon.

"That's true," Rosa nodded. "We did find a way though, didn't we?"

"Yes, my bear cub danced," Dickon said, with a flash of pride. "That last day, in the meadow, Nounou really danced. It would have been all right."

"And it wasn't cruel, either," Rosa said. "That was the best of all."

They smiled at one another.

All the same, it would be lonely without him. It was lonely already. Dickon looked up at the mountains.

"We don't have to stay here now," he said, his voice rough. "We can take the mule and go."

Rosa pushed back her hair.

"Let's wait a bit longer," she said. "Just in case..."

Dickon shook his head.

"Nounou won't come back now," he said.

"No," said Rosa, with a sigh. "No ... I suppose not."

But they waited just the same, sitting close together and looking, from time to time, towards the path he had taken.

The sun was beginning to dip behind the mountain when they heard the sound of horse's hooves. Rosa jumped to her feet and began to run towards the cleft in the rocks.

Then Sebastien was there, gathering her up into his arms and covering her with kisses, while Bruno, who was smiling for once, clapped Dickon heartily on the shoulder.

Later, much later, when they had heard all that there was to tell, Bruno said that if only they had come sooner he would dearly have liked to settle his own score with the Bear Catcher, who had tricked Marie into telling him when Sebastien and Rosa would be away from the valley. But Sebastien said it was just as well as it was, and after giving Dickon a mighty hug, declared that a tumbling act with a flute player was sure to be better than a tumbling act with a dancing bear, and besides, he went on, it was his opinion that this bear had fully earned its freedom by what it had done that day. To which Bruno agreed, especially since, as he said, the bear had always refused to dance. Hearing this, both Rosa and Dickon opened their mouths simultaneously, and then, thinking better of it, closed them again and said not another word on the subject of dancing bears.

Dickon, seeing that he was to stay with them after all, was heart glad, for even without the bear cub, he thought the life of a tumbler's musician would be better than any other he could imagine, especially since it meant that he could be with Rosa.

And thinking of how he would earn enough money to pay back Jacob when he saw him at the next Southwark Fair, and have silver for Ann as well, perhaps, he took out his flute and began to play a cheerful tune as they left the mountain clearing and started their journey back to the valley.

I am free. The mountains are mine once more. The little beast with two legs does not lead me with a rope, and no longer must I do his bidding, for no longer does he have command over me.

Now I am alone and I wander where I will ... over this mountain ... over that. I am returning to the place where I was born, for the time of whips and blood is over and my time has come.

HIPPO ANIMAL

Have you ever longed for a puppy to love, or a horse of your own? Have you ever wondered what it would be like to make friends with a wild animal? If so, then you're sure to fall in love with these fantastic titles from Hippo Animal!

Owl Cry
Deborah van der Beek
Can Solomon really look after an abandoned baby owl?

Thunderfoot
Deborah van der Beek
When Mel finds the enormous, neglected horse Thunderfoot, she doesn't know it will change her life for ever...

Vanilla Fudge
Deborah van der Beek
When Lizzie and Hannah fall in love with the same dog, neither of them will give up without a fight...

A Foxcub Named Freedom
Brenda Jobling
An injured vixen nudges her young son away from her. She can sense danger and cares nothing for herself – only for her son's freedom...

Goose on the Run
Brenda Jobling

It's an unusual pet – an injured Canada goose. But soon Josh can't imagine being without him. And the goose won't let *anyone* take him away from Josh...

Pirate the Seal
Brenda Jobling

Ryan's always been lonely – but then he meets Pirate and at last he has a real friend...

The Dog with the Wounded Paw
Brenda Jobling

When Emma sees Buster in the street she knows he needs help. But is it too late?

Animal Rescue
Bette Paul

Can Tessa help save the badgers of Delves Wood from destruction?

Take Six Kittens
Bette Paul

James and Jenny's dad promises them a pet when they move to the country. But they end up with more than they bargained for...

Take Six Puppies
Bette Paul

Anna knows she shouldn't get attached to the six new puppies at the Millington Farm Dog Sanctuary, but surely it can't hurt to get just a *little* bit fond of them...

HIPPO GHOST

Secrets from the past. . . Danger in the present. . .
Hippo Ghost brings you the spookiest of tales. . .

Castle of Ghosts
Carol Barton
Abbie's *bound* to see some ghosts at the castle where
her aunt works – isn't she?

The Face on the Wall
Carol Barton
Jeremy knows he must solve the mystery of the face on
the wall – however much it frightens him...

Summer Visitors
Carol Barton
Emma thinks she's in for a really boring summer, until she
meets the Carstairs family on the beach. But there's
something very *strange* about her new friends. . .

Ghostly Music
Richard Brown
Beth loves her piano lessons. So why have they started to
make her *ill*. . . ?

The Ghost Twin
Richard Brown
James will never forget Joe. But his twin was killed in a
road accident three years ago. He's never coming back...

A Patchwork of Ghosts
Angela Bull
Who is the evil-looking ghost tormenting Lizzie, and why
does he want to hurt her. . . ?

The Ghosts who Waited
Dennis Hamley
Everything's changed since Rosy and her family moved house.
Why has everyone suddenly turned against her...?

The Railway Phantoms
Dennis Hamley
Rachel has visions. She dreams of two children in strange,
disintegrating clothes. And it seems as if they are trying
to contact her...

The Haunting of Gull Cottage
Tessa Krailing
Unless Kezzie and James can find what really happened in
Gull Cottage that terrible night many years ago, the
haunting may never stop...

The Hidden Tomb
Jenny Oldfield
Can Kate unlock the mystery of the curse on Middleton
Hall, before it destroys the Mason family...?

The House at the End of Ferry Road
Martin Oliver
The house at the end of Ferry Road has just been built.
So it can't be haunted, can it...?

Beware! This House is Haunted
This House is Haunted Too!
Lance Salway
Jessica doesn't believe in ghosts. So who *is* writing the
strange, spooky messages?

The Girl in the Blue Tunic
Jean Ure
Who is the strange girl Hannah meets at school – and
why does she seem so alone?